MANDIE®
AND THE
NEW YORK SECRET

Mandie® Mysteries

MANDIE®
AND THE
NEW YORK SECRET

Lois Gladys Leppard

BETHANY HOUSE PUBLISHERS
MINNEAPOLIS, MINNESOTA 55438

Mandie and the New York Secret
Copyright © 2003
Lois Gladys Leppard

MANDIE® and SNOWBALL® are registered trademarks
of Lois Gladys Leppard.

Cover illustration by Chris Dyrud
Cover design by Eric Walljasper

Published by Bethany House Publishers
A Ministry of Bethany Fellowship International
11400 Hampshire Avenue South
Bloomington, Minnesota 55438
www.bethanyhouse.com

Printed in the United States of America by
Bethany Press International, Bloomington, Minnesota 55438

ISBN 0-7642-2639-8

For
CAROL JOHNSON,
who accepted the first MANDIE BOOK twenty-one
years ago, and who has held Mandie by the
hand all these years.
And to all the wonderful people at
Bethany House Publishers who accompanied
Mandie on the way.
With much love and many thanks.

About the Author

LOIS GLADYS LEPPARD worked in Federal Intelligence for thirteen years in various countries around the world. She now makes her home in South Carolina.

The stories of her mother's childhood as an orphan in western North Carolina are the basis for many of the incidents incorporated into this series.

Visit her Web site: *www.Mandie.com*.

Contents

"To thine own self be true,

and it must follow, as the night the day,

Thou can'st not then be false to any man."

—William Shakespeare,

Hamlet (Polonius) Act 1, Scene 3

Chapter 1 / New York at Last!

The train pulled into the station in New York and stopped with a sudden lurch. Mandie Shaw straightened up in her seat and recaptured her white cat, who had managed to escape her with the motion.

"Snowball, you have to behave now. We're going out there into a noisy, overcrowded street," she said as she secured his red leash and bent to pick up her small bag.

"I'll help you with him," Celia Hamilton said as she stood up.

Mrs. Taft, Mandie's grandmother, looked back as she started down the aisle of the train car and said, "Amanda, be sure you hold on to that white cat now."

"Yes, ma'am, I will," Mandie replied, following Celia.

Joe Woodard and his parents, Dr. and Mrs. Woodard, came along behind them.

"Yes, I don't want to have to search for that cat in this big city of New York," Joe said with a grin as Mandie glanced back at him.

As they all got off the train, Dr. Woodard led the way out of the depot and hailed a public carriage.

While everyone waited inside the carriage, he went back to pick up the luggage.

"It won't be long now until I find out what the secret is that Jonathan said he had found," Mandie said to her friends.

"It must be something important for him to send you a message by wire to the depot back home," Celia said.

"Remember he said in the wire to hurry up and come on up to New York, that he had found a secret," Mandie told her. "And he doesn't know how close he came to missing me with the message."

"He knew you were coming on up to visit while your mother and the others were at his house," Joe said.

"But he didn't know when we would get back to my house from visiting my Cherokee kinpeople," Mandie replied, rubbing Snowball's fur to calm him down as he tried to get away from her again.

"I hope my mother has already been shopping when we get to Jonathan's house so I won't have to spend so much time buying clothes," Celia said.

"Yes, and my mother, too," Mandie agreed. She glanced at her grandmother, Mrs. Taft, and Joe's mother, Mrs. Woodard, sitting across from them, but they were deep into their own conversation and were not paying any attention to the young people.

Finally, Dr. Woodard and the driver came back with all their luggage and loaded it, and then they started on their way to Jonathan Guyer's house. Even though Mandie had been to the big city of New York once before, and that was for Thanksgiving in 1901, it was now June of 1903, and everything seemed new to her again. The carriage driver drove as though he were going to a fire and ignored the pedestrians who scampered out of his way as they crossed the streets before them. She held tightly to Snowball as the vehicle swayed.

When the carriage turned into the driveway of the Guyer mansion and stopped under the portico, Mandie remembered seeing it that first time and being absolutely speechless to learn that Jonathan lived in such a huge stone building. And as it had happened the other time she came to visit, the door opened and the butler came out to assist with the luggage, only this time she knew the man's name.

"Good morning, Jens," Mandie greeted the man as he assisted Mrs. Taft out of the carriage.

Without even looking at her, the proper butler replied, "Good morning, Miss Amanda." After Mrs. Taft was safely out, he turned to help Mrs. Woodard alight.

As Mandie waited for everyone to go inside the house, Mrs. Yodkin, the Guyers' housekeeper, appeared at the doorway. "Please come in," she told Mrs. Taft and Mrs. Woodard. Looking back she added, "All of you, please come into the house."

Mandie looked around as they stepped into the parlor that opened off the portico. There was no sign of Jonathan or his father, or Mandie's mother and the others who had come to New York ahead of them. Then she realized the others were also wondering where everyone was.

"Is Jonathan at home?" Mandie asked the housekeeper.

Mrs. Yodkin stopped and looked directly at Mrs. Taft and Dr. and Mrs. Woodard, who had been following behind her. "I regret that there is no one here at the present. Everyone has gone to visit friends in Long Island. Since we did not know your arrival date, Mr. Guyer left the message that if you arrive in his absence you are to make yourselves comfortable."

"Gone to Long Island?" Mrs. Taft repeated, frowning. "Probably to see the Fredericksons."

"Yes, madam, that is where they went," Mrs. Yodkin replied. "Now, if you will all come with me, I will show you to your rooms." At that moment Monet, the French maid, came into the room. "And Monet here will show you young people to your quarters," Mrs. Yodkin added.

Mandie thought, *What a difference in our servants and the Guyers'*. The ones in the Shaw household were treated with friendliness and love. These people seemed to be cold and detached from the world.

When Mrs. Yodkin started toward the door, Mrs. Taft just stood there, frowning. "When is everyone coming back?" she asked.

Mrs. Yodkin stopped and looked back. "Mr. Guyer said they would return tomorrow," she explained. "They only left yesterday." She continued walking out into the huge hallway. The others followed.

Mrs. Woodard looked at Mrs. Taft and said, "That will at least give us time to recuperate from that long train journey."

"Yes, but we don't have that much time to stay here," Mrs. Taft replied.

Monet finally spoke to the young people. "If you will come this way, I will show you your rooms," she said, turning the other direction in the long hallway.

The girls and Joe looked into the rooms they passed along the way. Mandie remembered seeing the huge library they passed, the music room with two baby grand pianos in it, a formal drawing room, and another parlor. Huge double doors set in the mahogany wainscoting were closed.

They reached the carved stairway, split in the middle and rising on either side to meet a balcony above. At the bottom of the stairs, Monet stopped and, pointing to a door with glass windowpanes in it, said, "I remember you do not like the lift. Do you still not like it?" She waited.

"Let's walk up," Mandie and Celia said at once and then grinned at each other.

Joe spoke up as they continued up the stairs. "I should just ride up and let y'all walk. What are y'all going to do when you find a place that only has elevators and no steps?"

"Oh, Joe, there won't ever be such a place," Mandie replied, holding on to Snowball as he tried to get down.

"I wouldn't guarantee that," he replied.

Monet went ahead of them, threw open the door to a room on her right, and said, "Here is the room for you." She looked at Mandie and then added, "Box of sand for cat is here."

"Oh, thank you," Mandie replied, looking into the room.

"And you will be next door," the maid told Celia, pushing open the door to the next room. Then quickly stepping across the hall, she opened another door and said, "And this will be your room." She looked at Joe.

"Thank you," Joe said.

Jens and another servant came along the hall-way with their luggage, and Mandie, Joe, and Celia stepped out of the way while it was deposited in their different rooms. Monet stood there waiting until this was accomplished. Then she said, "We will have luncheon ready in thirty minutes." Then she turned and walked back down the hallway, following the other servants.

"Thirty minutes," Mandie repeated. Turning to Joe, she said, "I'll meet you back out here in fifteen minutes."

"All right," Joe agreed, going into the room he had been given.

The girls found their rooms had an adjoining bathroom, and each bedroom had a huge four-poster bed. Mandie put Snowball down at last, and he immediately found the sandbox.

"Why don't we just share one room?" Celia asked. "Then we can talk."

"Yes, I was going to suggest that," Mandie agreed. "We can use this one because Snowball's sandbox is in here. Now, let's hurry and change clothes so we can go talk to Joe." She looked at the small china clock on the mantelpiece.

At that moment there was a slight knock on the door, and Zelda, the other maid, stuck her head in. "I come to unpack zee clothes," she said in her foreign accent.

"Oh, hello, Zelda," Mandie greeted her. "Let us just get something out right now to change out of these traveling clothes, and then you can hang everything up."

"Yes," Zelda agreed, going to open the trunk the men had put in the bedroom.

"They put my trunk in the other room, and you can hang everything up in the wardrobe in there, but I am going to sleep in here with Mandie," Celia explained.

Zelda looked at her, smiled, and said, "I know.

House too big, dark, empty." She began unpacking Mandie's dresses.

While Zelda was doing that, Mandie went into the other room with Celia to help her open her trunk and get something out to change into.

The girls actually made the change and were out in the hallway within fifteen minutes. Joe was already sitting on a settee near his doorway. Various pieces of furniture and lamps were placed all along the corridors of the Guyer mansion.

"Y'all made it," he said, standing up and grinning.

"Let's just sit here a minute," Mandie told him as she and Celia sat down and he sat beside them.

"It's a long way back to the parlor, so we can't sit too long," he reminded them.

"I know," Mandie replied. "I just wanted to ask, without anyone around to hear, do y'all think we could start trying to find out what this secret is that Jonathan said he had found?"

"Oh, Mandie, how can we look for something when we don't even know what we are looking for?" Joe asked with a loud sigh.

"Well, in the message Jonathan said he had *found* a secret, so it must be something you can see," Mandie explained.

"But this house is so big we'll never be able to *see* any secret that Jonathan might have found without his help," Celia reminded her.

"Anyhow, how can you *find* a secret?" Joe asked. "A secret is usually something someone knows or does that they don't want you to find out about."

"Joe, now you are getting complicated," Mandie argued. "You know Jonathan doesn't exactly use the same English we do, since we're from the south and he's here in the north. So he says things in a different way from us sometimes."

Joe suddenly stood up and said, "Anyhow, I think we'd better get started back to the parlor." Grinning at Mandie, he added, "We sure don't want to keep your grandmother waiting for her meal."

"Joe, that's mean," Mandie said, pouting as the three started down the hallway.

"Well, I could include my parents in that, too. They like their meals when they are hungry, and I imagine they are all awfully hungry by now," Joe said.

"I am hungry myself," Celia told them.

"Me too," Mandie added, walking faster down the long hallway. "And I have to bring something back for Snowball. I hope nobody lets him out of our room while we're gone."

"All of the servants know you brought him, so I imagine they'll be watching out for him," Celia said.

Suddenly Mandie stopped and asked, "Where are we going? No one told us where to go." She looked at her friends with a frown.

"Hmm," Joe said, running his long fingers through his unruly brown hair. "I suppose we should go back to the parlor where we came in."

"There will probably be someone in there to tell us where we are expected to eat," Celia added.

"This house is just too big," Mandie complained as they walked on down the huge staircase they had come up before.

"Now I believe we go down this hallway," Joe said, motioning to the left.

The girls stood there looking at the different corridors branching off from the bottom of the steps.

"Yes, I believe you are right," Mandie agreed.

With Joe leading the way, they eventually found the parlor again. Mrs. Taft and Mrs. Woodard were sitting there talking as Dr. Woodard roamed the room looking at the fine objects on shelves and in cabinets, which had evidently been collected from various countries and which looked very expensive.

"We finally got back," Mandie said, going to sit on a settee near the two ladies. Joe and Celia joined her. "Grandmother, I thought your house was big, but this one is absolutely too big. You have to walk miles to get from one place to the other."

"Yes, I know," Mrs. Taft replied. "I see no reason to display one's wealth in that way."

Before Mandie could reply to that, Dr. Woodard settled down in a nearby chair and said, "But it is good exercise, especially after eating all the rich food served in such households."

Mandie smiled at him and said, "But I like to get my exercise outdoors where I can walk and walk. And as far as I remember, New York is not very walkable."

Joe grinned at her and said, "Is there such a word? Walkable?"

Mandie blew out her breath and said, "Oh, you know what I mean. It's so crowded here in New York, you can't walk down a street without getting bumped into and having to get out of someone's way." And then grinning at him, she added, "But I do love New York. I'm just not used to it."

Mrs. Yodkin came to the doorway just then and said, "Ladies and sirs, if you will all follow me please. We have the meal ready."

She led them to a small dining room at the back of the house that had French windows overlooking an enclosed garden. As everyone sat down at the table, she explained, "We did not open the windows because Master Jonathan's dog is out here in the garden and he would be likely to come into the house."

Mandie quickly leaned forward to look out one of the windows. "Yes, there he is, sitting there watching us," she said. "So Jonathan still has him." The big white dog was looking at her.

"Yes, miss, and he has become one of the family," Mrs. Yodkin said with a smile. "Now, if you are all ready, we will serve the food," she added to Mrs. Taft and Mrs. Woodard.

Mrs. Taft nodded, and Mrs. Woodard said, looking around the table, "I believe we are ready and probably hungry, too, after that fare on the train."

Mrs. Yodkin stood back, watching and supervising the other servants as they poured coffee, brought steaming food to the table in expensive china bowls, and checked to see that everyone had napkins and the proper silverware, all of which was already on the table when they sat down. Mandie smiled to herself as she realized the servants were only going through a memorized ritual for serving meals.

Finally, as everyone began eating, Mandie looked down the table at her grandmother and asked, "Do you have plans for us today, or are we just going to sit around and rest?"

Mrs. Taft laid down her fork and replied, "Mrs. Woodard and I have been discussing that, dear, and we have decided that we will just recuperate from our journey today." Smiling at Dr. Woodard, she added, "And the doctor thought that was a good idea."

"A good idea except that I need to get some exercise," Dr. Woodard replied. Looking at the young people, he said, "Thought maybe you all would be interested in a long walk this afternoon."

"Oh yes, sir," Mandie quickly replied with a big smile.

"Yes, sir," Celia nodded.

"Count me in," Joe told them.

"Then we'll just get out and go," Dr. Woodard replied. Turning to his wife and Mrs. Taft, he added, "Are y'all sure you don't want to come with us?"

"No, I'll get enough exercise just walking around this huge house," Mrs. Woodard replied.

"And I will get my exercise tomorrow when we all go shopping," Mrs. Taft said. Looking at Mandie, she said, "Now, Amanda, you are not to go off out of this yard without an adult with you. Is that understood?"

"Yes, ma'am," Mandie replied. Then she asked Dr. Woodard, "Do you think we could take Jonathan's dog with us for that walk? As far as I remember, Whitey loves exploring streets and sidewalks."

"Yes, I suppose we could. But, Joe, you will have to be responsible for the dog and see that he doesn't get away from us," the doctor answered.

"Yes, sir, Whitey will remember us, I think, and there won't be any problem controlling him on the streets," Joe said.

Looking at her grandmother, Mandie said, "I should take Snowball with me so he can get some exercise. I can put him on his leash!" Then smiling, she added, "And Whitey will behave with Snowball around. He's afraid of the cat."

Everyone laughed. Even the prim servants smiled.

Turning back to her friends, Mandie said, "Maybe we could explore the garden to see if we can find Jonathan's secret."

Joe blew out his breath, frowned, and then smiled as he said, "Amanda Elizabeth Shaw, how are we going to find Jonathan's secret when we don't even know what it is we're looking for?" He spoke so loudly he caught his father looking at him.

"Joe, let's keep this a secret among us three," Mandie whispered. "We don't want grown-ups messing in our business, do we? We'd never solve a mystery with them in on it."

Celia smiled at Mandie and asked, "And what are we going to do when we get to be grown-ups? I'm already fifteen, and you soon will be."

"Oh, that's a long time away before we get to be grown-ups," Mandie quickly told her. "And tell me one thing. Why should we we stop tracking down mysteries and secrets when we do grow up? I'm sure I'll have the same curiosity about things that I do now."

"That's the truth," Joe said, grinning. "You'll never outgrow it, Mandie."

Celia thought about that, frowned, and then said, "I'm not sure what I will do when I am grown. It might be fun to act like the dignified young ladies that Miss Hope and Miss Prudence are trying to make out of us at their school."

"No, that would be too restrictive," Mandie protested. "I want to do whatever I want to do, not what someone else thinks I should do."

"Wait till you get to college," Joe said, looking at both girls. "Then you will have to settle down, at least a little."

"Oh, Joe, you go to college and I can't see that

you have changed any," Mandie told him. Then, lowering her voice so her grandmother wouldn't hear her at the other end of the table, she added, "I am still thinking about asking Grandmother to take all of us back to Europe next summer for our graduation from the Heathwood's School. We could at least have one last fling." She grinned at Celia and Joe.

"Well, I suppose, if you call that a fling," Joe said.

"I would call it very educational and a whole lot of fun," Celia added.

"When I catch the right time and place to ask Grandmother about this, I'll let y'all know," Mandie promised. She hurried to finish eating. She was anxious to walk the streets of New York right now.

Chapter 2 / Plans

The weather was warm for June in New York. Mandie was glad Dr. Woodard led them over to Central Park to walk beneath the trees. Dozens of people sat in the shade there, reading, talking, or just relaxing and watching strollers go by.

Dr. Woodard, always the friendly gentleman, nodded, tipped his hat, and smiled as they passed several ladies who smiled at them.

As soon as they were out of hearing, Joe quickly asked, "Did you know those ladies?"

Dr. Woodard grinned at him and said, "Why, no, never saw them before in my life. It doesn't hurt anyone to smile, does it?"

Joe looked at Mandie walking by his side, with Celia in step with Dr. Woodard. "You don't smile at anyone in this park," Joe warned her with a frown. "This is New York and you never know what reaction you might get from a stranger in this town."

"I can assure you, if someone smiles at me first I'll smile right back," Mandie replied with a frown. Looking at Dr. Woodard, she added, "Just like your father does."

"But you are a pretty young lady, and it's dan-

gerous for young ladies to be friendly with stran-
gers," Joe said. He held the end of the leash for
Whitey as the dog trotted along and smelled of
everything.

"If you couldn't protect me and Celia, then
Whitey can," Mandie replied. She set Snowball down
to walk at the end of his red leash.

"Oh, Mandie, this is getting to be a silly conversation. Let's change the subject," Joe told her.

"Like Jonathan's secret," Mandie said, making
sure Dr. Woodard couldn't hear her.

"All right, then, Jonathan's secret," Joe agreed
with a shrug. "But there's nothing we can do about
that until Jonathan comes back home."

Slowing down to let Dr. Woodard and Celia walk
a little ahead, Mandie whispered to Joe, "I have
decided we ought to search his room to see if we can
find anything relating to a secret."

"Oh no, not me," Joe quickly told her. "I am not
searching anyone's room for any reason, much less
for something that we don't even know what it is.
Besides, I think it would be dishonest."

"We wouldn't be doing any harm," Mandie
argued. "And he will never know we did it."

"Harm?" Joe exclaimed. "It would not be right
to go through another person's personal things."

Dr. Woodard and Celia both suddenly stopped
and looked back. They were a few feet ahead of
Mandie and Joe.

"Are y'all tired already?" Celia asked.

"Tired? Oh no," Mandie quickly replied, walking
faster. "Just dillydallying." She smiled at her friend.

They had come to the edge of the park. Dr.
Woodard looked ahead, then glanced back to say, "I
see a place over there that looks like it might have

coffee. What do y'all say?"

Mandie quickly said, "I say yes, sir." She could see a small sidewalk café across the street. She picked up Snowball as he tried to run ahead.

"Yes, sir," Celia added.

"Coffee would be nice. Maybe they have some chocolate cake, too," Joe said.

They crossed the street and sat down at one of the little tables on the sidewalk, in the shade of a huge awning. Mandie held Snowball in her lap.

"I believe coffee is all we should have, and that rather quickly," Dr. Woodard told the young people. "I imagine those servants back at the Guyers' house will insist we have afternoon tea when we return."

"Yes, sir, and they'll have something sweet with it," Mandie agreed.

"Then let's hurry and get back," Joe said. He held the end of the leash as Whitey sat by his chair.

The waiter came and Dr. Woodard ordered. He quickly returned with four cups of hot coffee and placed them on the table.

"Dr. Woodard, when are you going to see Dr. Plumbley?" Mandie asked as she sipped the hot coffee.

"I'll have to see if Lindall Guyer has anything planned for us first before I contact Dr. Plumbley," the doctor replied.

"I'd like to see him, too, but Jonathan may keep us busy whatever time we aren't shopping with our mothers," Mandie said.

Dr. Plumbley was from back home in Franklin, North Carolina. He had come to New York years ago to get his medical education and had stayed to build up a well-known practice.

"I hope my mother has done a lot of the shopping already and that we don't have to spend too much of our time in the stores," Celia remarked.

"Maybe my mother has already bought whatever we need," Mandie said, picking up her cup of coffee. "That is one thing I love about my grandmother. She doesn't waste time shopping. She can always go directly to whatever it is she's looking for and that's it."

Dr. Woodard pushed back his chair and stood up. "If everyone is finished, I believe we should get back to the house now," he said.

The three young people quickly rose. Joe held Whitey's leash and Mandie carried Snowball.

"I am really surprised that your grandmother agreed to come to the Guyers' house," Celia remarked as they started down the sidewalk behind Dr. Woodard.

"I am, too, but it was the only solution to our being able to go visit my Cherokee kinpeople first and then come up here," Mandie said. "If Grandmother hadn't agreed to come with us to visit the Guyers, then we would have had to come on to New York with my mother and your mother and Uncle John. I was surprised, too, that she agreed to come."

"I'm glad you finally got that quilt mystery solved," Joe told Mandie.

"So am I," Mandie agreed. "My grandmother figured out why I wanted to visit my Cherokee people, and she was anxious to know what it was all about. I explained it all to her the night we got back home."

Dr. Woodard slowed down to look back. "Now, y'all must get a move on. Otherwise it's going to be suppertime before we get back to the Guyers' house." He smiled at the three.

"Yes, sir," Joe replied, walking faster and holding on to the dog's leash as Whitey suddenly decided to rush ahead.

"Oh, we have to get back for tea," Mandie agreed. She and Celia caught up with the doctor.

They did make it back just in time for tea. Mrs. Yodkin was waiting for them in the parlor. She spoke to Dr. Woodard. "The ladies are still retired. Shall we send word up that tea is about to be served, sir?"

Dr. Woodard hung his hat on the hall tree just outside the doorway and replied, "Yes, please, that will save me a journey through all those hallways to tell them." Then he stepped back inside the parlor.

"Yes, sir," Mrs. Yodkin replied as she turned to leave the room. "We will have tea ready in fifteen minutes, sir." She went out into the hallway.

Mandie, Celia, and Joe found seats around the parlor and sat down to await the afternoon tea. Mandie set Snowball down, and he jumped up onto a stool and curled up.

Joe reached down to unclip Whitey's leash and said, "Maybe I should put Whitey back out in the yard now." He looked at his father, who had sat in a large upholstered chair.

"Yes, I believe you ought to do that," Dr. Woodard replied. "I think it would be better if he was not present when the tea and goodies arrive."

Joe stood up, smiled at the girls, and said, "I'll be back as soon as I can find my way through all the hallways to the back door." He left the room with Whitey following.

Dr. Woodard looked across the room at the girls and asked, "And what do you young ladies plan on doing with the rest of your vacation after we go home next week?"

"Are we going home next week, then?" Mandie asked.

"Yes, your grandmother is not too anxious to stay here very long, and it seems she is expecting her friend Senator Morton to come to your house in Franklin late next week. And of course I have to get back to my patients," Dr. Woodard explained.

"Yes, sir," Mandie replied. "Grandmother had told me she was expecting Senator Morton and that maybe we would visit the Pattons in Charleston. I'm not sure what my mother is planning, but I do know that my grandmother is usually the boss."

"What about you, Miss Celia?" Dr. Woodard asked.

"My mother always says it's better not to plan too far ahead because something else may come up that we had rather do. As far as I know, she will go on home when we return to Franklin and allow me to stay and visit at Mandie's house for a little while." Glancing at Mandie and smiling, she added, "So I suppose it's up to Mandie as to what we will be doing. She usually has some good plans."

"It would be nice to visit the Pattons. I love the ocean down there," Mandie said. "However, I may resist, because I don't want my grandmother always leading everyone around on a string." She grinned at the doctor.

Joe stepped into the parlor at that moment and heard the comment. "And how long is that string?" he asked, grinning at Mandie as he sat down nearby.

Mandie laughed and said, "Not very long when my grandmother begins pulling it."

Mandie suddenly realized she did not know what Joe's plans were. She frowned as she asked, "When do you have to return to college?"

Joe sighed deeply and said, "I am going back early, probably in about two weeks. You see, I'm still trying to catch up and get ahead with my studies since I did not have the exact requirements for entrance to the college."

"Joe!" Mandie exclaimed.

Joe frowned and said, "I'm sorry." Then he quickly added, "But you'll have Tommy Patton to help you solve mysteries if you go to his house in Charleston. And if you don't, you can always get Polly Cornwallis to help you." He grinned mischievously at her. Polly Cornwallis lived next door to Mandie in Franklin and was forever chasing Joe when he came to visit.

"Polly Cornwallis! Never!" Mandie declared. "Besides, she's always afraid of everything. And Tommy Patton is not dependable. Soon as we find a mystery, he wants to run off to something else before we even solve it."

"But you always have Celia," Joe said, winking at Celia with a smile.

Before Mandie could reply, Celia quickly said, "Yes, I always follow Mandie through her mysteries and right on into her troubles sometimes."

"We haven't been involved in any bad trouble really," Mandie said. "Think of all the good we've done by solving a lot of our mysteries."

At that moment Mrs. Taft and Mrs. Woodard came into the parlor.

"Oh dear, don't tell me you are all off on another mystery," Mrs. Taft said as she sat in a nearby chair.

"That's what it sounds like," Mrs. Woodard added with a smile at Mandie as she sat near Mrs. Taft.

"No, ma'am, we haven't found a real mystery.

Maybe when Jonathan comes home we'll find one,"
Mandie said. She didn't want her grandmother to
know about the secret Jonathan had wired that he
had uncovered. She had hidden the message in her
purse.

Monet, the parlormaid, came in with the tea tray
on a cart. Mrs. Yodkin followed closely behind, over-
seeing the serving.

Joe stretched to see what was on the trays. "Ah,
there's lots of goodies," he whispered to the girls.

"Including chocolate cake," Mandie added.

As soon as everyone was served, Monet left the
room.

"If you should want something else, please ring
the bell. The rope is over there," Mrs. Yodkin told the
ladies as she motioned toward a heavy plush rope
hanging at the side of one of the draperies.

"Thank you," Mrs. Taft said.

Then Mrs. Yodkin went on out into the hallway,
and the adults began their own conversation among
themselves.

The young people ate for a few minutes as
though they were starved. Then Mandie asked her
grandmother, during a lull in the adult conversation,
"Will we be going shopping in the morning, or will
we wait for Mother and Celia's mother to come back
and go with us?"

"I thought we'd just run down to a couple of
stores in the morning and get whatever we need,
and then when Elizabeth and Jane and John return,
we won't have so much shopping left to do," Mrs.
Taft replied with a smile at the girls. "What do you
young ladies think?"

"Oh, that's the very thing to do," Mandie agreed.

"Yes, ma'am, I'd like to go with y'all since we

don't know when my mother will be back," Celia replied.

"Then you girls plan on it," Mrs. Taft said.

Looking at her son, Mrs. Woodard said, "And, Joe, you might as well come with us in case we find something for you to wear. You're growing so fast I'm not sure I could fit you."

Joe shrugged his shoulders, sighed, and finally said, "Yes, ma'am."

Mandie knew Joe did not like to go shopping.

"Remember what I said about my grandmother," Mandie whispered to her friends. "She won't waste time in the stores like my mother does."

Dr. Woodard spoke up. "Since you ladies are going shopping tomorrow morning and we don't know when the others will come back from Long Island, I suppose I should just go on and look up Dr. Plumbley." He grinned at his wife. "I'm certainly not going shopping with you ladies."

"Yes," Mrs. Woodard agreed. "That is a good idea."

"I was hoping I could go visit Dr. Plumbley while we're here," Mandie said, looking at her grandmother.

"We'll shop first and get that out of the way," Mrs. Taft said. "Then I will see that you get an opportunity to visit with Dr. Plumbley before we go home." She smiled at her granddaughter.

"Thank you, Grandmother," Mandie replied. "Please remember you said that when my mother gets back and wants to spend all our time in the stores." She grinned at her grandmother.

"I'm sure Elizabeth will understand," Mrs. Taft replied.

As soon as tea was finished, Mrs. Taft and Mrs.

Woodard decided to sit in the back garden for some fresh air. Dr. Woodard joined them. The young people followed them outside but drifted away toward the far end, out of hearing of the adults. Mandie fastened Snowball on his leash to a stake in the garden.

Sitting on a long stone bench by the fence, Mandie said, "Remember I suggested searching Jonathan's room for clues to his secret?"

"Yes, and I refuse to do that," Joe reminded her.

"Oh no, Mandie, I couldn't do that," Celia protested.

Mandie blew out her breath and argued, "But we won't disturb anything. He won't ever know we've been in his room."

"No, and I mean the answer is no, so just count me out of that," Joe emphatically told her.

"And me too," Celia added in a whisper.

Mandie jumped up and paced around the bench. "All right, all right," she said. "I'll do it by myself. However, y'all could help me look through some of the other rooms."

"But, Mandie, what are we looking for?" Celia asked.

"Well, something concerning his secret. I don't know just what, because I have no idea as to what the secret is," Mandie said, frowning as she thought about it. "However, we might find something mysterious somewhere or other."

"Mandie, Jonathan will be back home tomorrow," Joe reminded her. "It's best if we just wait and talk to him."

"In the meantime we don't have anything to do," Mandie complained.

"Just for the rest of this day. Tomorrow we go shopping," Celia said. "And I'm sure when Jonathan gets home we won't have a spare moment, because he is on the go all the time."

"Remember Dr. Woodard said we would be going home next week," Mandie reminded her friends. "Therefore, we shouldn't waste a minute of our time here in New York."

"I'm not wasting any time. I'm just plain tired after that long train trip," Joe said, stretching out his long legs in front of him.

"And tomorrow we'll feel as though a cyclone has hit us when we get into that shopping district, all those women snatching and grabbing everything in the stores and pushing and shoving you out of their way. Makes me tired just thinking about it," Celia said, shrugging her shoulders.

"Oh, Celia, that won't happen with Grandmother in charge," Mandie said. "She knows how to handle all that. Besides, we won't be going into very many stores. She has certain ones that she prefers and never wants to go exploring into the others."

"You two country girls need to get out of the country more often," Joe teased them.

"Joe Woodard, I am a country girl and proud of it," Mandie said. "As far as I am concerned, an occasional trip to New York is plenty."

"And since we live close to Richmond, an occasional trip to Richmond is plenty for me," Celia added.

"You girls need to think about your future," Joe told them. "You can't live in the country forever. You'll have to get out into the world and go to college. In fact, that is not too long off. Next year when you graduate from that boarding school in Asheville, you are both going to have to spread your wings." He grinned at them.

"Just because you picked that college in the big city of New Orleans is no sign I'm going to pick one in such a big city," Mandie replied. "I'm sure there are smaller colleges and some in country towns, too."

"Your choice will depend on what exactly you want to study," Joe reminded her.

"You know the answer to that very well," Mandie said, getting up to walk around the flowers. "Grandmother keeps reminding me that I have to have an education to handle all the business that I will inherit someday from her and my mother and Uncle John." She stopped to look at Joe and added, "Unless I could figure out some way to get disinherited." She laughed loudly.

"I'm glad I have no such burden to bear," Joe quickly told her, also laughing out loud.

Celia looked at her two friends and said, "Well, I hope to someday marry a man who will take care of all that for me, because I, too, am the only heir right now."

"That's the solution," Joe teased. "Mandie, you should just get married and let your husband handle all the business matters."

Mandie stomped her foot as she stopped to look at him. "I certainly don't want a husband who would be handling my life for me."

Joe sobered up and said, "I agree. A marriage should be a partnership." And then whispering to Mandie, he added, "And that's just what we'll make ours."

Mandie felt her face flush, and she turned to Celia and said, "Let's go to our room and rest awhile." She stooped to pick up Snowball.

Celia stood up and Joe joined them.

"That sounds like a good idea," he said. "We need a little rest before dinner."

Mandie led the way back into the house. When the three found their way upstairs to their rooms, Joe went inside his and closed the door. Mandie took Snowball inside hers and Celia followed. The cat jumped up onto the bed.

"I do believe I am a little tired," Celia said, plopping into a large cushioned chair. Then she stood up. "In fact, I think I'll go into my room and lie down for a few minutes," she added.

"All right," Mandie agreed. "Just in case I fall asleep, I hope you don't and will let me know when it's time to go down for supper."

"Of course," Celia agreed, going through into the next room and closing the door.

Mandie quickly looked around her room. She didn't intend lying down. She was going snooping into Jonathan's room if she could find it. Who knew what she might find.

Chapter 3 / A Discovery

Mandie left Snowball curled up asleep on her bed and quietly opened the door and slipped out into the hallway, making sure she closed the door behind her. Holding her breath and hoping that Joe would not come out of his room, she quickly tiptoed down the long hallway. Pausing at the top of the curved staircase, she asked herself, "Now, which way would Jonathan's room be?"

When she had visited the Guyers for Thanksgiving in 1901, she didn't remember Jonathan ever telling her and her friends exactly where his room was. He had said the wing in which they were staying was the guest wing. She looked ahead and saw a turn in the corridor, which meant there must be another wing around the corner.

The hallway was dark even though there were lamps lighted along the way. The mahogany wainscoting covered the bottom half of the walls, and a dark flowered wallpaper reached from there to the tall ceiling. Small settees, chairs, and tables were scattered along every hallway in the mansion that she had been in. Every time she thought about that, she smiled to herself and said, "They have so much furniture it won't all fit into the dozens and dozens of rooms."

She quickly walked on down to the corner in the hallway. Looking down another corridor, she could see there was a cross hallway intersecting this one. This place was like the streets outside in New York: corners, intersections, and no directional signs to tell her whether she was headed toward the front or back of the house. All the doors along the way seemed to be closed. She stopped and decided to open a door and if possible look out a window to see where she was.

"Please don't squeak," she whispered as she turned a knob and slowly pushed a door open, revealing a bedroom. The draperies were drawn, making the room dark and musty-smelling.

"This must be a guest room," she muttered to herself as she stepped inside. She walked over to a window, found the pull for the draperies, and gave it a yank. The draperies opened, revealing a large window with the outside shutters closed, which made it impossible to see out.

"Oh, shucks!" Mandie said, slightly stomping her foot on the thick flowered carpet. She turned to glance around the room. It looked similar to the one she had been given, with a tall four-poster bed, wardrobe, bureau, washstand, and several chairs, all of which must have cost a fortune.

Stepping back into the hallway, Mandie tried to remember how many turns she had made since leaving her room in order to figure out which side of the house she was in. But then she realized she had not even looked out the window of her room. Therefore, she did not know what was below it.

"Well, I suppose I'll just keep going," she decided.

Continuing down the hallway, she finally came to a large open area with a skylight overhead and steps going down in the middle of it. Walking around the circular hallway, she searched for doors and found one huge double door halfway around from the head of the stairs. She paused to look at it.

"That looks like a door to a parlor or something, not a bedroom," she said to herself.

Stepping over to the door, she turned the handle and gave a push. It wouldn't open. Then, looking closely, she found it was a sliding door and not one that could be swung open. Grasping the handle, she gave a shove and the door slowly moved on its track. As the opening widened, she squeezed through into the room.

"Well!" she said in surprise as she gazed at the skylight in the ceiling and the dozens and dozens of chairs and tables placed in rows about the room. Walking on into the room, she saw a large stage at the far end, with a huge maroon-colored velvet curtain drawn across it. Looking around she added, "Not a single window in this room."

Suddenly realizing she had been gone from her room for quite a while, she decided she had better work her way back before someone missed her. She stepped into the hallway, closed the sliding doors, and started back the way she thought she had come.

She had not gone very far before she realized she was in a corridor that she had not come through. Stopping to think, she said to herself, "Oh well, I suppose if I just keep going I'll eventually get back to my room."

She continued down the dimly lit hallway. Some of the doors here were slightly open. When she stepped inside a room to look around, it was evidently being used, but no one was there at the moment. There were toiletries on the bureau, the wardrobe door was slightly open, revealing clothes hanging inside, and the room smelled of perfume.

"Probably one of the servants' rooms," she whispered to herself as she started to step back out into the hallway.

Suddenly someone came rushing in, and they collided in the doorway.

"Oh, I'm sorry," Mandie muttered, moving back to straighten her skirt and then look at the other person.

"Excuse me, miss," the girl standing there said in surprise.

It was Leila, the young German maid who took care of the bedrooms in the mansion. She smiled as she pushed back her white cap on the top of her reddish blond hair.

"Please forgive me. This must be your room. I was looking for Jonathan's—" Mandie began.

Leila interrupted. "Master Jonathan's room. Come, I show you." She stepped back out into the corridor.

Following the girl down the long hallway, Mandie was trying to compose herself after being caught in someone's room. Evidently the girl did not think it strange that Mandie wished to see Jonathan's room.

Leila seemed to be going around in circles through the hallways, and as Mandie followed her she wondered what she would say to the girl when they finally came to Jonathan's room. Would the maid go on her way and leave her there to go into the room and explore? What would she say to Leila for an explanation as to why she wanted to see his room?

Suddenly Leila stopped in front of a door halfway down one of the hallways and turned to Mandie and said, with an indication of her hand, "Here is Master Jonathan's room." She smiled at Mandie and stood waiting.

Mandie frowned as she looked at the door and said, "So this is Jonathan's room." She was nervous and wouldn't look directly into Leila's eyes.

"*Ja,* miss, is his room," Leila replied.

Mandie glanced up and down the long hallway and asked, "Where are we? Is this the front of the house, or where?"

Leila replied, still smiling, "*Nein,* miss. Back of house, it is."

Mandie did some quick calculations. "Oh, so it is above the back garden," she replied thoughtfully. "Can we look out and see?"

Leila shook her head, still smiling, and answered, "Nein, miss. Master Jonathan, he locks the door when he goes away."

Mandie was surprised at that. "Locks the door?" she repeated.

Leila pulled a large key ring full of keys out of her apron pocket, held them up, and said, "But I have key."

"In that case, could you unlock the door so we could look out the window in there?" Mandie asked.

Leila shook her head again and said, "Nein, miss. I open only to clean, and it has been cleaned today."

"Well, I suppose I had better find my way back to my room," Mandie said with disappointment, wondering how she would ever remember where his room was. She turned back the way they had come.

"Miss, we go this way," Leila quickly told her, pointing in the other direction.

"But we came from that direction," Mandie said, pointing back.

"Ja, but you not at your room when we start," Leila explained. She started walking as she said, "We go this way."

Mandie followed the girl. After three different turns at cross halls, they ended up in front of Mandie's room. Celia was standing there looking out the open door.

"Oh, Mandie, I was beginning to believe you must have been lost," Celia told her. "And it's time to go back downstairs."

As Leila went on her way, Mandie explained, "I was just walking around the hallways and got lost. Leila showed me the way back." She went on into her room. Celia followed and closed the door.

"Mrs. Yodkin has already been by to say it's time for us to go back down to the parlor. Dinner will soon be ready," Celia explained.

"All right. Soon as I wash my hands and brush my hair I'll be ready," Mandie said, going toward the bathroom door. Then looking back, she noticed Snowball was no longer on the bed. "Where is Snowball? I hope he didn't get out." She started looking around the room.

Celia laughed and said, "No, Mrs. Yodkin wanted to take him to the kitchen to feed him, but she seemed to be afraid of picking him up. So I went across the hall and asked Joe to take him down."

So Joe had gone down to the kitchen with the cat. Mandie hurriedly freshened up. She closed their door behind Celia.

"Did you go back in the other part of the house and get lost?" Celia asked as they hurried toward the staircase.

"Yes. I don't know exactly where I was. All the doors are closed. I looked in one room, but then all the outside shutters seem to be closed, so I couldn't tell where I was," Mandie hurriedly explained as they descended the steps. She cleared her throat and added, "I just wanted to see what else is in this house."

"Well, I'm glad that we have memorized the way to the parlor from our room and won't get lost when we're in a hurry, like now," Celia said.

At the bottom of the staircase, Mandie stopped and asked, "Did you tell Mrs. Yodkin I was not in our room but out wandering around somewhere?"

Celia laughed and said, "Of course not, Mandie. In fact, I didn't even mention your name to her. She just said it would soon be time for dinner and that she would like to take Snowball to feed him. She didn't come inside our room. Joe came in and got Snowball, and he didn't ask about you, either. He was in a hurry. He said he wanted to speak to his father about something if he got a chance before dinner."

Mandie blew out her breath and contined on down the hallway. "I'll sure be glad when Jonathan gets back home."

Celia looked at her as she walked fast to keep up. "Because of the secret he said he discovered. I'm getting more curious myself, wondering what would be important enough for him to send a wire to you."

Mandie laughed and replied, "Oh, but you forget. Money means nothing to Jonathan. There's always more in his father's bank. I just hope he hasn't forgotten about the secret by the time he comes back home. You know how he flits to one thing and then another. He's always busy with something going on."

"I know," Celia agreed.

As they turned the last corner in the hallway and came into the part where the parlor opened off it, Joe and Dr. Woodard were coming along from the other end.

"Just on time," Joe teased as they all stopped at the open door to the parlor.

Dr. Woodard went on inside the parlor, and Mandie and Celia caught up with Joe.

"You are almost late yourself," Mandie teased back.

"Y'all come on or we really will be late," Celia said, leading the way into the parlor.

Mrs. Taft and Mrs. Woodard were sitting near the fireplace, and Dr. Woodard had joined them.

When Mandie saw the fire, she was amazed that the Guyers would have one going in the month of June. But then she realized the huge mansion seemed to be cold, and she was glad she had on a long-sleeved dress.

"Did y'all have a nice rest after your walk?" Mrs. Taft asked as the three young people sat down on a settee near her.

"Yes, ma'am," Celia said.

"Grandmother, you should have gone with us," Mandie said. "We had coffee in a sidewalk café, just like those we saw when we went to Europe."

"Probably the one across from the entrance to Central Park, was it?" Mrs. Taft replied, looking at Dr. Woodard.

"Yes, ma'am, that was the one," he agreed.

At that moment Mrs. Yodkin came to the parlor doorway. Looking across the room directly at Mrs. Taft, she announced, "Dinner is served, madam."

Mrs. Taft immediately stood up as she replied, "Thank you, Mrs. Yodkin. We're ready."

As they all followed Mrs. Yodkin from the parlor, Mandie thought about her grandmother. Mrs. Taft always seemed to command respect and was always the one consulted in such cases. Somehow people got the impression that Mandie's grandmother was the boss. She grinned to herself as she thought, *They just don't know how much of a boss she is.*

After they were all seated at the table in the dining room and were served, Mandie decided to tell Joe and Celia what she had done that afternoon. She made sure the adults were engaged in their own conversation.

Sitting between Joe and Celia, Mandie whispered, "I have something to tell y'all."

Joe and Celia both immediately looked at her and then leaned forward to listen to whatever she had to say.

Glancing from one friend to the other, Mandie whispered, "I found Jonathan's room this afternoon."

"You did what?" Joe exclaimed, loud enough that Mandie saw her grandmother look down the table in her direction.

"Please don't talk so loud," Mandie told him.

"What have you been up to now?" Joe asked.

"I said I found Jonathan's room," Mandie repeated in a whisper.

"Mandie!" Celia exclaimed in a whisper.

"I hope you are not planning to search his room," Joe said, frowning at her as he bent closer to speak.

"It's locked," Mandie said.

"So you couldn't get in," Joe said, smiling at her. "That's good."

"Leila, the German maid, has the key to it. She carries a key ring just full of keys," Mandie explained.

"How do you know that?" Joe asked.

"Because I asked her where the room was and she showed me and said it was locked because she had already cleaned it today," Mandie explained, still speaking in a whisper.

"So that's where you went this afternoon," Celia said.

"If I can find out her schedule for tomorrow, I'm going to be around there when she opens the room to clean," Mandie told them.

"Remember we are going shopping in the morning," Celia reminded her.

"And Jonathan is coming home sometime tomorrow," Joe added. "Why don't you forget about this crazy idea of searching his room, Mandie?"

"I want to know what the secret is he has discovered," Mandie said.

"I don't think you'll find the answer to that by searching his room," Joe told her. "And he will be home tomorrow."

Mandie realized her grandmother was watching her and that she had not eaten one bite of food during the secretive conversation. She picked up her fork and dug into the mashed potatoes on her plate. She glanced at her friends' plates and saw that they had been consuming their food.

Mrs. Taft spoke from down the table. "Amanda, Mrs. Woodard and I have decided we will begin our shopping journey immediately after breakfast tomorrow morning, which I understand is served at eight o'clock. So you should all be ready to leave as soon as we have finished breakfast. We plan to be back by noontime."

"Yes, ma'am," Mandie replied, quickly swallowing her potatoes.

"Yes, ma'am," Celia added.

"And I'll be ready, too," Joe told her, looking at his mother.

"And I will be leaving then to go visit Dr. Plumbley and should return in time for the noon meal," Dr. Woodard added.

"Does anyone know yet when my mother and the others will be back from Long Island?" Mandie asked.

"Mrs. Yodkin knows the transportation schedules to and from Long Island and thinks they should return by noon," Mrs. Taft replied.

Celia and Joe both immediately glanced at Mandie. She sighed and said under her breath, "Oh well!"

The three of them knew Mandie would not have time to catch Leila and get into Jonathan's room.

"That will keep you out of trouble," Joe whispered, grinning at Mandie.

"Well, at least if he's here when we get back we can find out about this secret he discovered," Mandie said, frowning at her friends.

When the meal was finally over and everyone stood up to leave the room, Mandie suddenly remembered Joe had brought Snowball downstairs to eat.

"Where is Snowball?" she asked Joe as they followed the adults, who had walked out into the hallway and were going into the parlor for coffee.

"I took him to Mrs. Cook in the kitchen," Joe explained. "She said she would feed him."

"But, Joe, where is he now? Someone may have let him out," Mandie said, getting excited.

"I don't think so," Joe said. "You see, I fastened on his leash, and Mrs. Cook hooked the end of it to her cabinet door in the kitchen just in case he tried to get out."

"I think I'd better go get him," Mandie said and then added, "if I can find the way to the kitchen. I don't know why anyone would want such a monstrous house."

"I know the way," Joe said. "Go this way." He turned down the hallway in the opposite direction from the parlor.

"I hope you know the way. Wait a minute," Mandie stopped him. "I suppose I should tell my grandmother where we are going if we are not going to have coffee with them."

Joe stopped and said, "I almost forgot about that. No, let's go have that coffee first and then we can get Snowball."

"I suppose he can wait," Mandie agreed. Grinning at Joe, she added, "I don't think the possibility of chocolate cake can wait."

"Never," Joe replied.

"Yes, let's have our coffee and cake first," Celia said, smiling at them.

As soon as everyone settled down in the parlor, Mrs. Yodkin came in with Monet rolling the tea cart behind her. Joe stretched to glance at the contents on the tray, smacked his lips, and said, "I was right.

That's chocolate cake on there."

"You must have given Mrs. Cook a hint when you took Snowball back to the kitchen," Mandie teased him.

"Let's see, now. Come to think of it, I do believe she asked me if we like chocolate cake," Joe said, grinning at her.

Mrs. Yodkin watched as Monet served the coffee and cake. When they were finished, she turned to Mrs. Taft and asked, "Do you wish Monet to stay and replenish your cups, madam?"

"No, no, thank you, Mrs. Yodkin. We can take care of that," Mrs. Taft replied.

"Yes, madam. We will return later for the cart," Mrs. Yodkin replied. Then she followed Monet out of the room.

Mandie noticed again that Mrs. Yodkin had spoken to her grandmother for instructions, and she smiled.

"What is so funny?" Joe asked, watching her.

"Mrs. Yodkin treats my grandmother like she is the lady of the house," Mandie said, beginning to giggle and setting her coffee down as it sloshed in her cup.

"I noticed that, too," Celia said.

"I suppose your grandmother just looks like the lady of the house," Joe teased.

Mandie thought about that. Her grandmother had her own mansion and servants and was used to being the lady of the house.

Chapter 4 / Mandie's Escapade

After everyone had gone to bed that night, Mandie tried to stay awake until Celia fell asleep. She intended exploring the hallway to see whether Jonathan's room might possibly be unlocked. Celia seemed to be in a talkative mood, and Mandie pretended to be sleepy.

"What do you intend buying tomorrow?" Celia asked after they were in bed.

"I don't know," Mandie mumbled.

"If I see something I really want, I suppose I can go ahead and buy it. I think that will be all right with my mother," Celia said.

"Ummm," Mandie replied.

"Of course, I'll have to go shopping with my mother, too," Celia said. "And I have no idea as to what she will want to buy."

"Ummm," Mandie again mumbled.

"You sound half asleep, Mandie, so I'll shut up. Good night," Celia said, turning over on her side away from Mandie.

"Night," Mandie muttered as she turned over on her side of the bed. She kept listening for Celia to go to sleep. Celia seemed wide awake. And Mandie had to keep blinking her eyes to keep from falling asleep herself. She waited and waited.

The next thing Mandie knew, she suddenly sat up in bed. She had been sleeping. And Celia by her side was evidently sound asleep. She wondered what time it was. How long had she slept? Did she dare creep around the dimly lit hallways in the huge spooky mansion in the middle of the night by herself? And would she be able to find Jonathan's room?

Mandie pushed up in the bed to look around. The room was dark, but faint light filtered in through the sheer curtains from the moonlit sky outside. Snowball was sound asleep at her feet. Celia was still turned over facing the other side of the room, so Mandie couldn't tell whether her friend had opened her eyes with the movement or not.

Suddenly she heard the faint chimes of the tall clock down the corridor outside and learned that it was actually five o'clock in the morning. Therefore the servants were probably up and around already, so she must hurry if she was going to look for Jonathan's room.

Slowly sliding down from the tall bed, Mandie stood up, grabbed her robe from a nearby chair, put it on, and without taking time to put on her slippers, she hurried barefooted over to open the door to the hallway. She looked up and down the corridor. There was no sign of anyone. Quickly stepping out of the room, she quietly closed the door and then crept down the hallway, being careful not to collide with any of the furnishings sitting about in the dark.

Mumbling quietly to herself, she tried to retrace the way she had gone to the room yesterday, or rather the hallways Leila had brought her down, because that was the shortest distance to Jonathan's room.

Suddenly, turning the corner into a cross hall, Mandie spotted Leila going down it ahead of her. She quickly ducked behind a small settee sitting nearby and peeked over the back of it until she finally saw Leila turn left at the next cross hall. She watched a few minutes and then continued on. She went in the opposite direction from that taken by Leila.

As she silently walked on, the hallway grew darker and darker, and then she realized the lamps along the way were not burning. With the doors to the rooms all closed, the corridor didn't get any light. And she almost passed a room that had the door open. She stopped and looked. *This must be Jonathan's room,* she thought as she slowly, quietly stepped inside. The shutters on the windows were closed, and the room was so dark she could barely see the furniture. She could tell there were objects on the dresser and the desk in the corner. Someone was using this room. She bent to look closely at whatever was there. She found cuff links in a glass dish on the bureau.

"At least I know this room is being used by a man," she decided to herself.

Opening the wardrobe door, she saw clothing hanging inside that confirmed that. Even in the darkness she could tell there were pants there.

Suddenly the door to the hall was quietly closed and she could hear a key turning in the lock. Her heart almost jumped out. She could not get out. And whoever locked the door had only paused to do that and was probably long gone down the corridor.

"Oh, why didn't I yell when they locked the door?" Mandie moaned to herself as she paced the floor of the room. "How will I ever get out of here?"

The room seemed to be darker than ever with the hall door closed. She had to feel her way around, touching furniture and stumbling into things. She tried the door but it wouldn't budge. And this room was probably so isolated that no one would ever hear her if she tried yelling. However, Celia would miss her. But on the other hand, Celia would not have known where she had gone. And this house was so big it would take someone a long time to locate her. She stumbled into a footstool in the dark and sat down on it to think.

Her grandmother was going to be furious with her if she didn't show up for breakfast. Mrs. Taft had told them all to be ready to go shopping right after the morning meal. And since no one knew where Mandie was, they would all waste time trying to find her.

She sat there for a long time thinking about what she could do. Then she heard a key being inserted into the lock of the hall door. She stood up and rushed to the far side of the room, trying to hide. She bumped into furniture, and putting her hand out to keep from falling, she felt what must be a doorknob. Quickly running her fingers over it, she realized it was actually a door. Hastily turning the knob, she pushed and was amazed to find it opening. She almost fell into the next room. Or whatever was beyond. Stepping inside, she quietly closed the door just as she heard the door to the hallway being opened.

Blowing out her breath for a moment, Mandie glanced around in the darkness and was surprised to see this was a bathroom. Feeling around the wall, she searched for another door. Finally her hand touched another doorknob. Pushing that door open, she found herself back out in the main hallway.

Her knees trembled and she almost lost her breath as she tried to hurry down the hallway before whoever had gone into the room came back out and saw her. She didn't look back until she reached the cross hall.

Leaning against the corner of the wall, she finally caught her breath. Trying to stay behind a chest standing there, she looked back. Then she almost lost her breath again as she saw Jens, the butler, come out of the room, lock the door, and continue down the hallway away from her.

"Oh, how awful!" she exclaimed to herself. "That must be Jens's room! If he had caught me, I just would have died right there on the spot." She blew out her breath, straightened her long robe, and silently stomped her bare feet.

Pushing back her long blond hair, she took a deep breath and hurried back in the direction of her room.

As she opened the door, Celia, already dressed, greeted her. "Oh, Mandie! Where have you been? It's time to go downstairs for breakfast." She frowned as she looked at Mandie.

Mandie threw off her robe and raced to the wardrobe to pull down a dress. "I just went . . . for a . . . a walk," Mandie muttered as she began hastily dressing. "And . . . got lost."

"I hope your grandmother is not furious with us for being late," Celia told her. "Remember, she told us to all be ready to go shopping right after breakfast."

"I know, I know," Mandie replied, buttoning her shoes and rushing over to the bureau. She picked up her brush and brushed her hair. "I'm ready, I'm ready," she said, looking around the room. "Where is Snowball?"

"Leila came and got him to take him downstairs to feed," Celia replied, hurrying over to the door and opening it. "Come on, Mandie. Let's go." She paused to look back.

"I'm coming," Mandie replied, rushing behind her into the hallway. Glancing at the door across the way, she asked, "Have you seen Joe this morning? Has he already gone downstairs?"

"Yes, he knocked on our door to say he was going ahead a while ago," Celia said, leading the way down the corridor to the staircase.

Mandie couldn't decide whether to tell her friends about her escapade. She wasn't sure what their reactions would be, due to the fact she had intruded into the butler's room, of all places. Joe would probably give her down the country about it. And it kinda hurt when he scolded her. Others' criticism just floated away, but his mattered.

"Come on, Mandie," Celia called from the bottom of the steps. "What's wrong with you being so slow? Are you all right?" She watched as Mandie caught up with her.

"Oh, I'm all right, Celia," Mandie replied, hurrying on down the corridor with her friend. "I'm just thinking about something."

"Well, I can tell you, that something had better be breakfast, because I don't want to incur the wrath of your grandmother to start off the day," Celia replied.

Mandie grinned at her as they walked on and said, "Oh, Celia, my grandmother is not that bad. All you have to do is smile at her and make her think you are agreeing with everything she says."

"Mandie!" Celia exclaimed.

They met up with Joe coming into the main hallway from a side corridor. "Well, well, you girls finally made it," he teased. "I was beginning to think I'd have to go get y'all." He walked along with them.

"That won't be necessary. We were looking for you," Mandie teased. "Why did you have to come downstairs so early?" She remembered Celia had said he had gone down earlier.

"So early?" Joe replied, grinning back. "Well, for one thing I had to go check on that white cat for you to be sure he was being fed and that no one would let him outside while we are gone shopping."

"That's nice of you to be so concerned about my cat," Mandie said, smiling at him.

"Oh, it's not your cat I'm concerned about. It's me. I don't want to waste my time chasing after him if he runs away," Joe replied, still smiling.

Mandie stopped in the hallway and said, "Joe Woodard, you don't have to chase after my cat. I can always find him myself," Mandie told him.

Joe also paused to look at her. Before he could reply, however, Celia looked back and said loudly, "Will y'all please come on? I'm hungry."

Joe grinned at Celia and quickly followed her to the parlor door. "Yes, and I'm hungry, also."

Mandie, reaching the door with him, said, "You are always hungry. However, I am hungry myself this morning. And I would advise you and Celia, too, to eat everything you can find on the table because, knowing my grandmother, when she goes shopping, that's all she does, shop. She never takes time to stop and eat. Therefore, I'd say we won't get another bite until we return here for the noon meal."

As they entered the parlor, Mrs. Taft and Dr. and Mrs. Woodard were rising from their chairs. Mrs. Yodkin, standing inside the doorway, had evidently just announced breakfast.

"We made it," Mandie whispered to her two friends.

"Just barely," Celia whispered back.

"Let's go," Joe whispered as they followed the adults to the dining room.

The three young people sat together down toward the other end of the table from the adults. Mandie was silent, trying to decide whether to tell Celia and Joe about her adventures that morning.

After they were served and had begun eating, Celia looked at Mandie and said, "You never did tell me where you went so early this morning."

Mandie swallowed a mouthful of coffee and said, "I just . . . walked around the hallways."

Joe immediately looked at her and said, "Now, I'd say that's not exactly an explanation. Have you been snooping around this big house?" He grinned at her and then added, "Like I have?"

"Oh, so you have been snooping," Mandie said, smiling at him. "And what did you see during your travels around the hallways?"

"Practically nothing but closed doors. These people really believe in keeping all the doors closed," Joe remarked, drinking his coffee.

"I know, and they are locked, too," Mandie agreed.

Quickly looking at her, Joe asked, "Locked? How do you know they are locked? Have you been trying to open all those closed doors?"

"No," Mandie quickly replied, sipping her coffee. "Not all of them, anyway."

"So which ones have you been able to open?" Joe asked.

Mandie frowned, looked up at him, and said, "Only one."

"One?" Celia repeated. "Mandie, you didn't go inside any of those closed rooms, did you?" She laid down her fork and looked at Mandie.

"Well, yes, but only one," Mandie replied. Then smiling, she added, "All the others were locked."

"And what room was it that you were able to go inside?" Joe asked.

"I don't know. It was dark and no one was in there," Mandie replied. "And it was a long way around the hallway from our room."

"Why didn't you turn on the light in it and see what kind of a room it was?" Joe asked.

"Turn on the light?" Mandie asked, puzzled.

"Of course. This house is lighted by electricity," Joe explained. "You know your room is, and all the rest is, too. It's not like back home, where the electricity has not been extended into the country yet."

Mandie quickly said, "Well, I knew that, of course, but I just didn't think about it." She was secretly thinking she would do just that next time.

Mrs. Taft spoke from up the table. "Amanda, you need to hurry up and finish so we can be on our way."

"Yes, ma'am," Mandie replied and quickly began eating the food on her plate.

Celia and Joe also finished their food.

Shortly thereafter, as everyone rose from the table, Joe asked, "And where exactly was this room you went in? I didn't find any unlocked doors along the way when I went down to the kitchen."

"I'm not positive," Mandie replied as the three of

them followed the adults out of the dining room. "I just walked down the hallway from our room and then turned into a cross hall, I think. This house is so big and so confusing to find my way around in it." She had quickly decided she would not tell Joe exactly where she had gone lest he figure out it was the servants' rooms, as it must have been.

Mrs. Taft looked back and said, "You all be at the front door in the parlor in fifteen minutes. We will be leaving then." She continued down the hallway.

"Yes, ma'am," the three replied.

When everyone gathered in the parlor a few minutes later, Hodson was there, ready to drive them in Mr. Guyer's carriage.

"Leave me at Dr. Plumbley's first," Dr. Woodard was telling the man.

"Yes, sir, that I will," Hodson agreed. "And when shall I return for you, sir?"

"Don't worry about that," Dr. Woodard replied. "I will ask Dr. Plumbley to drop me off here after our visit together."

Mandie heard that and said, "Oh, Dr. Woodard, if Dr. Plumbley brings you home and we have come back from shopping, please ask him in so I can see him."

Dr. Woodard smiled at her and replied, "Of course, Miss Amanda. In fact, I have cleared it with the housekeeper for Dr. Plumbley to have the noon meal with us here if everyone is back."

"We will be back by then," Mrs. Taft spoke up. "We don't have much shopping to do."

"Maybe my mother and the others will be back by then, too," Mandie said.

Everyone piled into the huge fancy carriage, and a little while later Hodson stopped in front of a small brick building downtown in New York. Mandie was not familiar with the city and had no idea where they were exactly. But there was a shingle hanging over the doorway: *Dr. Samuel Hezekiah Plumbley.* She smiled as she read it, proud of her old friend from back in Franklin, North Carolina.

After Dr. Woodard left the carriage, Hodson continued traveling downtown into the shopping district. Once in a while Mandie would see something that she remembered from her previous visit to New York, but it was mostly a busy, jumbled-up mess of buildings, carriages, pedestrians, and now and then a motorcar. And once again she thought, *How could anyone live in a place like this all the time?*

Suddenly Mrs. Taft spoke as the carriage slowed down. "Here we are. Hodson is going to wait for us around the corner. We won't be long, but we need to look for a new steamer trunk for you, Amanda."

As everyone stood up to get out, Mandie asked in surprise, "A new steamer trunk for me, Grandmother? But what will I do with it?" She followed her grandmother to the door of the carriage.

"Amanda, you will need a new trunk the next time we go to Europe," Mrs. Taft said. Looking back at Celia, she added, "I'm not sure whether your mother would want us to get one for you, too, Celia. I know Mrs. Woodard is getting one for Joe."

The three young people stopped and stood there, looking at the lady.

"To Europe? Grandmother, are we going to Europe again?" Mandie asked.

"Of course," Mrs. Taft said, looking back as Hodson assisted her and Mrs. Woodard in descending from the carriage.

The three young people hurriedly followed.

"But when are we going to Europe, Grandmother?" Mandie asked as she managed to stay right behind Mrs. Taft.

"I didn't know we were going back to Europe," Celia said.

"Neither did I," Joe added. "I wonder when this decision was made."

"We have had plans to return to Europe for a visit ever since you all went with me before," Mrs. Taft explained as everyone assembled in a group on the sidewalk.

"But when?" Mandie insisted on knowing.

"We'll have to make a decision on that soon, but while we're in New York we can go ahead and purchase the new trunks," Mrs. Taft turned around to say.

Mandie waited for Mrs. Taft and Mrs. Woodard to move ahead of them, and then she turned to her friends to whisper, "I have not asked her yet about going to Europe for our graduation present next summer. Therefore, she must be making plans of her own, plans that involve all of us, and we need to find out what it's all about."

"Yes," Celia agreed. "However, she has probably already talked to my mother or she wouldn't be buying a trunk for me today."

"And my mother evidently knows about it, too," Joe added.

Mandie glanced at her friends and said, "You know my grandmother. She is always in charge. Now all we have to do is find out what her plans are and decide whether we want to go along with them or not."

Her friends agreed.

Chapter 5 / The Storm

The young people followed Mrs. Taft and Mrs. Woodard into a huge store that seemed to sell everything. The ladies went straight to the section that sold trunks. And there were trunks of every shape and size and price.

Mandie and her friends looked over the assortment, and when Mrs. Taft made a choice Mandie noticed that it must have been the highest priced trunk in the collection.

"I think this one will do very well, as far as handling on and off the ship, and will also hold enough clothes for every occasion while we travel," Mrs. Taft said, examining the construction of the trunk she had selected. Turning to Mandie, she said, "Amanda, would you like this one? What do you think?"

Mandie had never been asked for her opinion before on such a purchase, and she frowned as she looked at the trunk. Then, smiling at her grandmother, she replied, "Grandmother, you are the expert. Whatever you decide will be all right with me."

"Fine, then we will order this one," Mrs. Taft

replied. Turning to Celia, she asked, "Do you think you would like one just like Amanda's? I could go ahead and order it for you. This store will ship the trunks to our homes, of course."

Celia didn't seem to know what to say. She looked at Mandie and then back at Mrs. Taft. "I'm sorry, Mrs. Taft, but I don't know what my mother would want to buy. As far as I am concerned, that one would be all right."

"Then we will order it for you," Mrs. Taft decided. "And I'm sure your mother will be pleased with it."

As Joe stood there listening and watching, his mother turned to him and said, "You will need a trunk of your own if you go to Europe, because I will not be going and I don't want you to take the only trunk I have at home in case I decide to go somewhere else while y'all are gone. Now, tell me what you would like."

"But I'm not sure I will be going with Mrs. Taft's group," Joe replied.

"Oh, but, Joe, you must go with us," Mrs. Taft said.

"Yes, I think you should go," his mother added.

"I don't know when they are planning to go, and I may be in extra classes at college and won't be able to leave," Joe said.

"Well then, Joe, we'll just arrange the journey for whenever you can go," Mandie spoke up.

"Yes, we'll take that into consideration when we make our plans," Mrs. Taft told him.

"All right, then," Joe finally said. Turning to his mother, he said, "Why don't you just pick out whatever I should have. I know nothing about steamer trunks." He glanced at Mandie and grinned.

Mandie grinned back and said, "It's time you learned."

Mrs. Woodard turned to Mrs. Taft and asked, "Could you give me some advice on what to purchase for Joe?"

"Of course," Mrs. Taft replied and then walked across the room to another stack of trunks.

The young people listened and watched as Mrs. Taft made recommendations to Mrs. Woodard and then Mrs. Woodard selected a trunk for Joe.

"Now that we're finished with the trunks," Mrs. Taft said, "we need to look at shoes. They have a much larger selection than we can find anywhere else."

So they followed Mrs. Taft onto another floor of the building and then into a section of nothing but shoes. Mandie had never seen so many shoes in one place. There were different styles, different leathers and fabrics, and also different colors.

And this department held shoes for everyone. So the young people had to try on shoes after shoes until the right fit was found in something they wanted to buy.

"Amanda, you are old enough now that I don't think your feet will grow any more, so I'd say it's safe to buy a few pairs to last until next year," Mrs. Taft told Mandie. "What would you like? We'll limit it to six pairs."

"Six pairs? Grandmother, what would I do with six pairs of shoes?" Mandie asked in amazement.

"You need shoes for different occasions," Mrs. Taft insisted, motioning to shelves holding every variety. "You need shoes to wear to school, school socials, walking shoes, slippers for formals, shoes for bad weather. Let's start over here with these plain ones for school." She picked up a black pair.

Mandie sighed as she followed her grandmother around the shelves. She had never seen so many shoes. And she could remember when she had only one pair of shoes, back when her father was living and she had not even known she had a living grandmother. They had lived in a log cabin at Charley Gap, and her father had worked hard on the farm for a living. *Oh, if he could only share in all this now.* She turned her back to her friends and wiped a tear from her blue eyes.

"I do believe it's raining outside," Mrs. Woodard said, looking out through the plate-glass window.

Mrs. Taft turned to glance out. "Indeed it is," she said. "And it looks awfully dark. This rain may last awhile. Luckily this store has a restaurant attached that we can go into for our noon meal if we have to."

"But weren't we expected back to dine with Dr. Plumbley at noon?" Mrs. Woodard asked.

"Yes, but I think we have a good enough reason to be excused from that," Mrs. Taft replied. Turning back to the young people, who were listening, she started naming other departments they needed to shop in while in that store.

Mandie didn't like not being able to see Dr. Plumbley as Dr. Woodard had promised. She caught up with her grandmother as the lady led the way across the floor. "But, Grandmother, we have the carriage. We wouldn't get wet, not much, if we got in the carriage and went back to the Guyers' house," she argued.

Mrs. Taft looked at her and said, "Amanda, this could turn into a storm, and I don't want to be outside if it does." She continued on across the store.

Mandie walked fast to keep up with her. "And

also, Mr. Guyer, Jonathan, and my mother and Celia's mother and Uncle John are all expected back about then, aren't they?" she asked.

"I believe so, Amanda, but they may have trouble getting back in the ferry if it storms," Mrs. Taft replied, still hurrying on to another part of the store.

Mandie dropped back with her friends and said, "My grandmother always has to have her way." She frowned.

"But in this case she may be right," Joe said. "We don't want to be caught out in a carriage in New York if a real storm comes up. Traffic can get jammed up and wrecks could occur."

"Oh, Joe," Mandie said. Glancing toward the large window across from them, she said, "It's only a little rainstorm out there, and besides, it may quit."

At that moment a deafening roar of thunder and a blinding flash of lightning outside caused them all to stop and look.

"Guess you're right," Mandie finally conceded as she hovered near her friends.

Mrs. Taft turned back to say, "Hurry on, now. We need to get to another part of this store where there's no window." She rushed on through the other shoppers who had also stopped to look outside.

Mandie overheard her grandmother and Mrs. Woodard talking as they walked on.

"I need to find the telephone in this store. I can call and let the servants know we are stranded and will be much later getting back," Mrs. Taft said.

"Yes, and I should leave a message for my husband," Mrs. Woodard agreed.

They finally found the office of the store, and Mrs. Taft used the telephone there to call the Guyer residence. Mrs. Woodard also added her message for Dr. Woodard. The young people stood by and tried to listen.

"Now that that's taken care of, we need to go to the restaurant. The lady at the desk explained which way to go," Mrs. Taft said.

Mandie suddenly remembered Hodson was sitting outside in the Guyer carriage, waiting for them in the storm.

"Grandmother, shouldn't we send word for Hodson to come inside out of the storm?" Mandie asked as she caught up with her.

"Yes, the lady at the desk will send someone out to speak to him. She said there is a small place where he is parked for him to get something to eat," Mrs. Taft explained. "Then when the storm has passed over he will come in here for us."

Mandie was relieved to hear that her grandmother had thought of the carriage driver.

The restaurant was not very crowded when they got there, but as soon as they were seated crowds started coming in. Evidently all the shoppers in the store had decided to eat at once.

The storm lasted for almost two hours, and by that time they had eaten and Mrs. Taft had finished shopping. Hodson came and got them after parking the carriage at the front door.

When they returned to the Guyer mansion, Mrs. Yodkin informed Mrs. Taft that Mr. Guyer had called from Long Island and said the ferry service was temporarily delayed because of the storm on the waters there.

"Mr. Guyer said they would try to get a ferry as soon as the storm is over and that you should all make yourselves at home in the meantime," Mrs. Yodkin told Mrs. Taft as they came into the parlor.

Mrs. Woodard looked around and asked, "And did Dr. Woodard return?"

"No, madam," Mrs. Yodkin replied. "The doctor called to say he would be staying with the other doctor for the noon meal and would return later this afternoon."

Mandie heard that and said, "And I missed seeing Dr. Plumbley."

Mrs. Taft and Mrs. Woodard had both walked across the room and sat down in front of the fire.

"The fire feels good after being out in all that wet," Mrs. Woodard remarked.

Mrs. Taft looked at Mandie and said, "We'll arrange to see Dr. Plumbley while we're here, so don't worry about it, dear."

Mandie smiled at her and said, "Thank you, Grandmother."

Mrs. Yodkin, waiting by the door, looked across the room at Mrs. Taft and asked, "Since the weather has jumbled up plans, should we serve tea early, madam? Perhaps it would be refreshing after traveling through the wet outside."

"Oh yes, thank you, Mrs. Yodkin," Mrs. Taft replied. To Mandie she said, "Amanda, if you and your friends want to get freshened up before tea, hurry and do so. I don't have the energy. I'll stay right here."

"Yes, Grandmother, and I need to see if Snowball is all right, too," Mandie replied, turning to leave the room. "Celia, Joe, are y'all coming? I'm going to the kitchen first."

"Yes, Mandie," Celia replied.

"Since I was the one who left him there, I'd better go, too," Joe said, and then grinning at Mandie, he added, "just in case he has managed to get loose and run off somewhere."

"Oh, Joe, that's not a laughable matter. I'd never find him in New York," Mandie replied, leading the way into the hallway.

"Or in this house, either," Celia added.

"You're right. He could get lost in this house and never be found," Mandie said seriously.

"Oh, you'd be able to find him. When he got hungry, he would meow loud enough to wake the dead," Joe said, laughing. "You'd hear him."

As they walked down the long hallway, Mandie said, "I'm glad that shopping with Grandmother is over with. Maybe my mother won't want to do much."

"I don't know what else your mother would want to buy. Your grandmother bought everything anyone could possibly need, or want, for that matter," Joe said.

"I'm glad she purchased things for me, too, so I won't have to spend a lot of time shopping with my mother," Celia said.

Joe found the way to the kitchen and pushed open the door. When he did, Snowball, tied behind a counter, immediately sent up a howl. Looking back at Mandie, Joe laughed and said, "I do believe he's in here."

There was no one in the kitchen. Mandie hurried behind the counter, untied Snowball's leash, and picked him up. "Oh, Snowball, just be glad you didn't have to go through what we've been through today," she told the white cat.

Joe went over to look out the window. "Whitey is on the back porch, so he wasn't out in the storm, either," he said. Looking at the girls, he asked, "Do you think it might be permissible to bring Whitey inside?"

"Oh no, Joe, not right now," Mandie quickly replied. "Remember we will be having tea, and that's food that he might want."

"Yes, you're right. I'll get him later," Joe said, turning back to the girls.

"Mandie, I'm going to our room to leave my hat and purse and wash my hands," Celia told Mandie.

"All right, I'll go with you. I suppose I'd better leave Snowball in our room until after tea, too," Mandie agreed.

"I need to freshen up, too," Joe said.

The three went upstairs to their rooms.

As Mandie hurriedly washed her hands and then brushed her hair, she wondered when she would get a chance to investigate the hallways again. According to Mrs. Yodkin, Jonathan had been delayed, so Mandie should have time to look around again if she could get away from her friends—or, on the other hand, maybe they would go with her up and down the corridors of the mansion.

Celia, using the other side of the bureau mirror to brush her hair, asked, "Mandie, when will we be able to settle things with your grandmother about that journey to Europe? There are other things I'd like to do."

"Other things? Like what?" Mandie asked, looking at her in the mirror.

"I'd like to go back to Charleston and visit the Pattons, and I know my mother has said she would like to, also, and maybe Robert would go, too," Celia explained. Robert was a friend who went to the boys' school near their school in Asheville.

"Oh, I see," Mandie said with a big grin. "Yes, I'd

like to visit the Pattons again, and I believe my mother intends doing that, but I don't know when. But I suppose since my mother and your mother and the Pattons are old friends, we could probably go just about any time and be welcome."

"What about your grandmother? She said that she expected Senator Morton to come to your house in Franklin when we return," Celia said. "Do you think Mrs. Taft intends taking him with us to visit the Pattons?"

"I don't know, but I do know my mother will have some say-so about some things we are planning," Mandie replied. "And Uncle John won't let my grandmother boss everyone else." She grinned at her friend.

Mandie's mother, Elizabeth, had married John Shaw after Mandie's father, Jim Shaw, had died. John was Jim's brother, and Mandie looked to him for support against any unwanted plans made by her grandmother, who was Elizabeth's mother.

"I sure am glad you have someone to look out for you," Celia remarked, grinning back.

Mandie threw down her brush and said, "Come on, we'd better go. I'm going to shut Snowball up in here." She looked at the white cat, who had curled up on the big bed and gone to sleep.

When they opened the door, Joe was waiting for them in the hallway.

"What have you two young ladies been doing all this time?" he asked teasingly.

Mandie led the way down the hallway toward the staircase and said, "Only necessary freshening up." Looking up at Joe, she added, "I'll be glad when Uncle John gets back. My grandmother seems to be making her own plans, plans that include everyone else."

"I realize that, but I also know how your uncle John can change some of her plans," Joe said laughingly as they descended the stairs.

"Joe, if we don't go to Europe until next summer, couldn't you go with us then?" Mandie asked.

"I suppose so, but I can't say for certain until later when I see what my academic schedule is for next year," Joe replied. Then, smiling down at Mandie, he added, "Of course, I'll do everything I can to arrange things so that I will be able to go with y'all. You can count on that."

"What about going with us if we visit the Pattons in Charleston after we get back home? Can you go with us then?" Mandie asked as they came to the bottom step and paused there.

"Mandie, I'll have to sit down and talk things over with my father. I believe he and my mother have some plans of their own," Joe replied. "However, I will go with you if there isn't a conflict in plans with them."

"Then we'll just ask your mother and father to go with us to Charleston, too. They are friends of the Pattons, also," Mandie said. "What I'm trying to do is figure out what we want to do and stay ahead of my grandmother with her plans."

"I know, I know," Joe agreed. "Come on. I'm hungry." He started on down the hallway.

"I believe I am, too, even though I did eat quite a lot in that restaurant," Celia agreed.

"And I would guess that Mrs. Yodkin has ordered chocolate cake for us," Mandie said with a big grin.

"In that case let's hurry," Joe said, walking faster down the long corridor.

When the three entered the parlor, Mrs. Taft and Mrs. Woodard were discussing future plans.

"Of course you and the doctor would be most welcome to go with us on our journey to Europe, you know," Mrs. Taft was saying to Mrs. Woodard.

The three young people sat down on a settee nearby and listened.

"Yes, and I thank you, but you know how doctors' work is. I don't know how much time the doctor can be away from his patients unless he gets another doctor to agree to look after them while he's away. And that new young doctor over at Bryson City expects sick people to come to see him rather than he go visit them."

"Yes, times are changing," Mrs. Taft agreed. "However, we ought to be able to work something out."

Mandie whispered to her friends, "Grandmother hasn't said when we would be going to Europe."

But then Mrs. Woodard was saying, "I certainly don't want you to plan anything because of us. If we are able to, we'd love to go, but on the other hand, go ahead and make your plans and we'll see what happens."

Mrs. Taft happened to glance up and saw the young people. "Of course you know I will have to get together with my daughter to settle on final plans for that journey to Europe. And I hope to be able to do that soon."

"Yes, I understand," Mrs. Woodard said.

At that moment Mrs. Yodkin came in with Monet following her, pushing the tea cart.

"Well, here's food," Joe said.

"Yes, and we can always discuss plans later," Mandie agreed.

Mandie was trying to decide if she would have time to explore the upstairs hallways or if her friends would agree to go with her before the Guyers and the others returned.

Chapter 6 / Waiting

As soon as tea was finished, Monet came back for the tea cart, with Mrs. Yodkin along to supervise. Mrs. Taft and Mrs. Woodard decided to stay in the parlor since Dr. Woodard would probably be back shortly.

Mandie looked at her friends and asked, "Would y'all like to go for a walk around the upstairs hall-ways since it's all wet outside?"

"If we don't take too much time, because my father should be back sometime this afternoon, and I'd like to discuss a few things with him," Joe replied.

"Yes, I need the exercise," Celia said, rising from the settee.

The three left the parlor and headed for the huge staircase at the front of the house. Mandie led the way as she tried to figure out which way they should go in order to pass by Jonathan's room. Even if the door was open, she didn't think she would stop to investigate with her friends along. She was sure they would object. However, if the door was open she could go on and have some excuse to backtrack.

"I've been thinking about that ferry from Long

73

Island, and I'm wondering if my mother and the others will be able to get back here today," Celia said as they climbed the long, curved staircase.

"I'm sure they will," Joe told her. "I think the ferry just got off schedule and the passengers are pretty well jammed up because of it. I would think the ferry will just keep on running back and forth to catch up."

"I hope they will get back today," Celia said.

"I do, too," Mandie said. "I want to get that shopping over with that I have to do with my mother. And I want to see Dr. Plumbley sometime or other before we go home."

"Yes, and I have to do some shopping with my mother," Celia reminded her as they came to the top of the staircase. "Now, which way do we go?"

"As far as I can tell, this hall goes clear around the house, with all these little cross halls off it," Joe remarked as they stopped to talk.

"I wonder what part of the house the family lives in, Mr. Guyer and Jonathan," Mandie said. "And also, where do the servants stay?"

"I have an idea the servants have rooms at the far end of the house on the inside hallway, which I found circles around the flower garden below. In other words, it's like a courtyard beneath their section," Joe said. "There's an inside stairway there that goes straight down into the back hallway where the kitchen is."

"That sounds complicated," Celia said with a laugh.

"There is also a huge ballroom of some kind at one end of the house," Mandie said.

"Yes, I found that, too," Joe said.

"Well, just what part of the house are our rooms in?" Celia asked.

"I believe we are just about in the middle. This house is very long," Joe explained. "And it also has a small third floor and a huge attic above that."

"I tried looking out a window in my room and also in Mandie's, and all I could see was trees and a rooftop below," Celia said.

"Oh, so that's what the view is from our rooms," Mandie said thoughtfully as she tried to envision where Jonathan's room was. "I've been meaning to look out to see where we are."

"Come on. I thought y'all wanted to walk," Joe told the girls as he started on down the hallway.

They walked up and down hallways and came to a balcony, beneath which was the glass room filled with plants and flowers.

"Oh, that's the room we found last time we were here, remember?" Celia told Mandie and Joe.

"Yes, I remember. Snowball loved that room because he could get in all those huge pots of plants," Mandie said.

"I just thought of something," Joe said. "I don't even know where my parents' room is, or your grandmother's, Mandie. Remember the house-keeper took them one direction and we went the other."

"You're right," Mandie said, walking over to a window on the outside wall and looking out. There was a small building below.

Joe followed and said, "That's where the butler lives now."

Mandie turned to look at him and asked, "Jens, the butler?"

"Yes, don't you remember Mr. Guyer gave him

the use of that place down there because of his little girl?" Joe told her.

"Oh yes, that's right," Mandie agreed. She remembered seeing Jens come out of the room that she had been trapped in that morning. So that was not his room, after all. But whose was it? It definitely belonged to a man, because what she had found in the wardrobe were men's pants. And if Joe was right about the servants' rooms being in the cross hall, then whose room was it? Could it possibly be Mr. Guyer's? He would probably have a whole suite of rooms somewhere.

"I think I'd better go back downstairs. My father might have returned by now, and I do want to speak to him about something," Joe told the girls, turning to go back the way they had come.

Mandie looked at Celia and asked, "Do you want to walk on around a little more?"

"I suppose so, but I am also wondering whether my mother and the others might be coming back soon," Celia replied.

"Just a couple more hallways," Mandie told her.

"All right," Celia agreed.

"Then I am going back. See y'all downstairs," Joe told the girls, and he walked back down the hallway.

The girls walked slowly on down the corridor they were in and then turned left into a smaller hallway. Then they made a few more turns into other hallways.

"I hope we aren't lost," Celia said with a smile. "We may never find the way back downstairs in time for supper."

"Oh, we can find our way back. We'll just go round and round, up and down these hallways, and we'll eventually get back to the staircase," Mandie said.

"But remember there is more than one staircase in this house," Celia reminded her.

"Well, if we go down any one of those, we will at least be on the main floor and then we can find the way back to the parlor," Mandie assured her. "The next staircase that we find we'll just go down it."

"I just can't imagine why anyone would want to live in such a mixed-up house," Celia remarked as they walked on.

Finally, Mandie spotted steps going down ahead. "There is a staircase right there," she said, pointing as they came closer. "Come on. We'll see where it goes."

Mandie noticed this staircase was plain and narrow and steep as they descended. Looking ahead, she said, "I believe we are coming down right by the kitchen."

"You're right," Celia agreed.

When they reached the hallway below, Mrs. Cook was just coming out of the kitchen and stopped to speak. "We will be having a big dinner tonight. Two doctors."

"Two doctors?" Celia asked.

"Dr. Woodard and Dr. Plumbley," Mandie said with a big smile.

Mrs. Cook nodded and said, "Yes." She went on down the back hallway.

Mandie looked at Celia and said, "Now, if I can remember the way to the parlor from here . . . I should have asked Mrs. Cook."

"Let's just keep trying different doors and halls real fast," Celia said, opening a door on their left.

"Oh, I'm lucky. I do believe this is the main hallway to the parlor."

"Yes, it is," Mandie agreed, leading the way down it.

They finally came to the door to the parlor. Mandie quickly looked as they stepped inside the room. There was Dr. Plumbley sitting in an armchair and talking with Dr. Woodard, who sat nearby. No one else was in the room.

"Well, hello, Miss Amanda," Dr. Plumbley said, quickly rising and coming to meet her.

Mandie rushed forward, grasped his hand, and said, "Oh, Dr. Plumbley, I'm so glad to see you." She smiled up at the tall black man whose education her grandfather had paid for many years ago. He was also the doctor who had saved her mother's life a long time ago when she had the fever and Dr. Woodard had exhausted his knowledge.

"It's a delight to see you, Miss Amanda."

Dr. Woodard spoke from his chair. "It didn't take much coaxing to bring him back with me for supper since we had missed out on lunch because of the storm."

At that moment Joe came into the parlor, saying, "I've been looking everywhere for you, Mandie, to tell you Dr. Plumbley was here." He sat on a chair near his father.

"We came down the back stairs," Mandie said. "I'm sorry. Let's sit down, Dr. Plumbley." They sat on chairs nearby. Mandie looked around the room and asked, "Where is my grandmother? And your mother, Joe?"

"Oh, they had gone to their rooms when I got back down here," Joe explained.

"They'll be back in time for supper," Dr. Woodard said.

Mandie turned back to Dr. Plumbley and asked, "How is Moses?"

"He's just fine," Dr. Plumbley replied. Moses was Dr. Plumbley's nephew.

Just at the moment Mandie opened her mouth to ask another question, the front door opened and Mr. Guyer came into the room. He paused, staring straight at the door to the hallway, and Mandie turned her head and saw her grandmother standing in the doorway. They both seemed to have frozen as they looked at each other.

Then suddenly Mr. Guyer moved aside and apologized to Mandie's mother, Elizabeth, Celia's mother, Jane, and Mandie's uncle John as they came into the room. "I apologize for blocking the doorway," he muttered.

Then Jonathan Guyer more or less pushed his way through the crowd into the room, glanced at Mrs. Taft, and came straight to Mandie, whispering, "Watch and listen."

Mandie and everyone else seemed at a loss for words as Mrs. Taft still stood in the doorway. Then Lindall Guyer hastened across the room, holding out his hand to Mrs. Taft and saying, "Welcome. It's been a long time." He smiled at her.

"Yes, but we don't have to dig up the in-between, do we?" Mrs. Taft replied as he continued holding her hand.

"Of course not," Mr. Guyer replied. "And I think we should all sit down and relax."

Jane Hamilton, Elizabeth Shaw, and John Shaw immediately went on through the parlor into the hallway, saying they needed to freshen up.

"Why don't we go outside for a little walk?" Dr. Woodard asked Dr. Plumbley, and they immediately left. Dr. Woodard nodded at Joe, motioning that he should also leave the room.

Joe stood up and said, "Come on, Jonathan, show us the way around this great big mansion."

Jonathan grinned at him and said, "Of course."

Mandie left the room with her friends even though she didn't exactly want to. She was dying to find out what was going on between her grandmother and Jonathan's father.

Out in the hallway, Jonathan said, "Come on. I'll tell you about the secret I found."

Mandie immediately forgot about everything else and quickly followed her friends.

Jonathan took them down the main hallway to a cross hall on the left and then opened a door on the right. "Come on. Let's go in here," he told them.

Mandie looked around as Jonathan turned on lights. The room was a library, and the books all looked very old.

"Just have seats there and I'll show you something," Jonathan said, motioning to chairs around a long mahogany table.

When everyone was seated, Jonathan turned to the bookshelves behind him and said, "These are all very old books and have been in here probably since before I was ever born. You see, my father inherited this house from his parents, and their furnishings are still in some of the rooms. This room, for instance, has never been changed as far as I know, and I'll show you the reason for my thinking that."

Mandie and her friends watched as Jonathan turned to a small ladder and climbed up it to reach the top shelf. He took out several books in the tightly packed shelf, laid them across some other books, and then reached inside the emptied shelf. He pulled out an envelope, came back down the ladder, and sat down at the table with the others.

"Now, I believe you are all going to be shocked by what I found in this envelope," Jonathan said, grinning at them as he slowly pulled out a handful of newspaper clippings and laid them on the table.

Mandie quickly leaned forward to look. "What is that?" she asked.

"Just some articles out of an old newspaper. Read what they say," Jonathan said, grinning again as he spread out the clippings.

Mandie and her friends leaned closer to read.

"But what could be so special about old newspaper articles?" Celia asked.

"Looks like gossip columns to me," Joe said.

"But read the names," Jonathan told him.

" 'The latest twosome on the town, Mary Elizabeth Ashworth—' " Mandie stopped, about to lose her breath as she recognized the name. "That's my grandmother's maiden name, there with your father's name!"

"Yes indeed," Jonathan said, watching everyone. "Read on."

" 'The beautiful heiress Mary Elizabeth Ashworth, with her steady escort, Lindall Guyer II, at the St. Patrick's Day Ball,' " Mandie read. She quickly flipped through the other clippings, which were all the same gossip column that seemed to follow every move her grandmother and Jonathan's father made. Looking at Jonathan, she said, "My grandmother and your father! But what happened to this romance?"

"I'm sorry, I don't know," Jonathan told her.

"This is all I've found so far. Evidently it broke up, because my father married my mother."

"So that is why my grandmother acts like she doesn't like your father whenever his name is mentioned," Mandie said, still shocked at the news.

"Maybe she was jilted by Mr. Guyer," Celia suggested.

"Or maybe Mrs. Taft jilted Mr. Guyer," Joe added.

"I don't know, but you all saw the looks on their faces when they met down there in the parlor a while ago," Jonathan said.

"But, Jonathan, didn't your father know my grandmother would be here when y'all came home?" Mandie asked.

"I don't know. I never heard anyone mention her name while we were gone," Jonathan said.

"Everyone certainly hurried out of the room," Celia remarked.

Mandie nodded and said, "Yes, like they knew something was going on." She tried to figure out their reactions.

"My father could possibly have known about this," Joe said. "He has known your grandmother, Mandie, for years and years and years. And—"

Mandie quickly interrupted as she took a deep breath and said, "I just remembered something. Uncle Ned said Mr. Guyer used to come visit at my grandmother's house when my grandfather was living. My grandfather died right about the time I was born, and I don't know if your father ever came back to visit after that, Jonathan." Uncle Ned was Mandie's father's old Cherokee friend.

"I don't suppose he did, because he had married my mother probably two or three years before your grandfather died," Jonathan figured.

"That solves some of the mystery, but why does Mrs. Taft always act like she doesn't like your father, Jonathan?" Joe asked.

"I haven't found out yet, but give me time. There's bound to be more information somewhere," Jonathan said.

"I overheard a remark that gave me the impression that my mother doesn't even know why my grandmother doesn't like your father, Jonathan," Mandie said.

"I was surprised that she agreed to come with us to your house," Celia said.

"I think there is some important reason," Jonathan said.

"This is going to be a strange situation while we're here together," Joe said. "What do we do now? Go back to the parlor together? We have to go to the dining room together to eat."

Mandie straightened up and smiled as she said, "We don't have to do anything. We can just act like nothing has happened."

"That's going to be hard to do," Celia said.

Jonathan gathered up the clippings, inserted them back into the envelope, and stood up. "I'll just put these back up there where no one will find them, and we can all come back in here and search the rest of this room. I didn't have a chance to do it before we went to Long Island." He climbed the ladder, replaced the envelope, and then hid it from view with the books he had removed.

All of a sudden Mandie started giggling, and everyone looked at her.

"Are you all right, Mandie?" Joe asked.

"I just think this is funny. I wish I could walk right

up to my grandmother and say, 'I know all about you and Jonathan's father,' " she managed to say between giggles.

Jonathan laughed and said, "We'll do just that before you all go home. In the meantime, maybe we'll find something else that will give us more information."

"Do y'all think Mrs. Taft may still be in love with Mr. Guyer?" Celia asked.

Everyone laughed. Then Mandie said, "I think it would depend on whatever broke up the romance in the first place. Just imagine my grandmother and your father, Jonathan."

"Yes, we were almost kin to each other," Jonathan replied with a grin.

"I intend staying away from both of them while I'm here," Joe said. Then he added thoughtfully, "In fact, I'm going to speak to my father and ask him if he knows why Mrs. Taft seems not to like Mr. Guyer."

"But, Joe, please don't give away our secret until we can look for more information," Mandie reminded him.

"I won't, but as you know, almost everyone will tell you that Mrs. Taft doesn't seem to like Mr. Guyer," Joe replied.

"And I'm also wondering why she agreed to come here with us to visit in Mr. Guyer's house," Mandie said. "And I intend finding out."

Everyone nodded in agreement.

And Mandie suddenly realized that if she had found Jonathan's room, she would not have found even a clue to his secret. Now that Jonathan had come home, they would all be able to help him in his search for more information regarding her grandmother and his father.

Chapter 7 / Decisions

Jonathan led the way to the parlor, where everyone gathered before mealtime. No one was in there except Dr. Woodard and Dr. Plumbley, deep in a conversation at one end of the room. And Lindall Guyer came in right behind the young people as they sat down near the doctors.

Mr. Guyer spoke to them. "I do hope you young ladies had something to do while we were gone." He sat in a chair by Dr. Woodard.

"Yes, sir," Mandie replied with a big smile. "My grandmother took us shopping this morning."

"And did you buy lots of pretty clothes?" Mr. Guyer asked.

"No, sir, we bought steamer trunks," Mandie explained.

"Steamer trunks? Then you must be going on a long journey," Mr. Guyer said.

"Grandmother says we're going back to Europe, but I don't know when," Mandie explained.

Dr. Woodard spoke to Mr. Guyer, "Dr. Plumbley here has been filling me in on some new treatments he has learned."

"Dr. Plumbley, that would be most interesting to

hear about," Mr. Guyer said, turning all his attention to the two doctors.

"Dr. Plumbley, before you get deep in conversation, Aunt Lou said if I saw you to tell you she sent her love," Mandie quickly said.

"Now, that's the best news I've had today. And how is that nice lady?" Dr. Plumbley asked.

"She's just fine," Mandie said. Aunt Lou was the housekeeper for her mother and Uncle John.

"I must get down to see all those friends, Abraham, Jenny, and Lou," Dr. Plumbley said, then turned back to talk to the other men.

Jonathan leaned over near Mandie, as they sat across the room from the adults, and said, "Do you suppose there's a romance going on between Aunt Lou and Dr. Plumbley?"

Mandie started giggling and put her hand over her mouth as she replied, "Oh, Jonathan, I had not even thought about that. They are about the same age, I believe, and they have known each other since way back years and years ago."

"And neither one of them is married," Joe added.

Celia whispered to Mandie, "I wonder where your grandmother is. I see Mrs. Yodkin headed this way, to announce supper I would imagine."

Mrs. Yodkin came to the door of the parlor and looked inside. Then without saying a word she turned and went back down the hallway.

"I hope she is not delaying supper," Joe said.

"She can't announce dinner until all the ladies have come back to the parlor," Jonathan explained.

"I wish they would come on back here so we can get this all over with," Celia remarked. "I think I'm hungry."

"Yes, so we can see how my father and your grandmother, Mandie, are going to behave in the same room," Jonathan said.

At that moment Jane Hamilton came into the parlor, followed by Mrs. Woodard, Elizabeth and John Shaw, and Mrs. Taft. The men stood up as the ladies entered.

Before anyone could speak Mrs. Yodkin came to the doorway again and announced, looking straight at Mr. Guyer, "Sir, dinner has been served."

"Thank you, Mrs. Yodkin. We'll be right in," Mr. Guyer said. As Mrs. Yodkin went back down the hallway, he added, "Ladies, shall we go dine?" looking directly at Mrs. Taft, who avoided his glance.

As Mr. Guyer led the way to the dining room, Mandie watched her grandmother. Mrs. Taft had immediately started talking to Dr. Plumbley and ignored Mr. Guyer. She seemed flustered, and Mandie had never seen her that way before.

With Mr. Guyer seated at the head of the table, the adults sat near him and the young people were placed down far enough that they could carry on their own conversation in low voices without being overheard.

"Your grandmother won't look at my father," Jonathan whispered to Mandie after everyone had been served.

"I noticed that," Mandie replied. "I wonder what they had to say to each other after everyone left the parlor when y'all came home, Jonathan."

"I'm afraid we'll never know," Jonathan said.

"Your grandmother seems to be awfully nervous," Joe said.

"She is not acting normal," Mandie decided.

"No wonder," Celia said. "Coming face-to-face

with an old beau from long ago would be unsettling."

"Well, I can't imagine how it would be," Mandie said. "Do you suppose we will have lots of old friends when we are as old as Grandmother?"

"Probably," Jonathan said.

Mandie was looking at her grandmother and saw her speak to Elizabeth. "I have bought the new steamer trunk for Amanda," she was saying. Turning to Jane Hamilton, she added, "I also purchased one for Celia."

Mrs. Woodard said, "I purchased one for Joe, also, just in case he is able to go with y'all."

Elizabeth looked at her mother and asked, "Steamer trunk for Amanda?"

"Yes, for our journey to Europe," Mrs. Taft explained.

"Mother, we haven't settled anything on that yet," Elizabeth replied.

"Neither have we, but I suppose Celia does need a new trunk," Jane Hamilton said. "I will reimburse you for it, Mrs. Taft, and thank you for saving me the trouble."

"So you are all planning to go to Europe," Mr. Guyer said.

"I certainly wish I could go with y'all, but I see no free time anywhere in the near future," Dr. Plumbley said.

John Shaw had been listening and now he said, "This journey may not be in the near future. It depends on when everyone will be free at one time." He turned to look down the table at Mandie and winked at her as he smiled.

Mandie smiled back. She knew what he meant. He was not going to let her grandmother make plans for everyone unless everyone wanted to go along with whatever it was.

"When did you plan on going to Europe, Mother?" Elizabeth asked.

"It would certainly have to be during the summertime because of school," Mrs. Taft replied. "And I was hoping we could make it this summer. I don't see why we couldn't."

"As far as Joe is concerned, the journey would depend on how long you plan to be away," Mrs. Woodard said. "He may have to return to college early because of the makeup courses he's trying to finish."

"And I will have to sit down and discuss plans with Celia before I would make any commitment," Jane Hamilton said.

"We could leave immediately after we return to Franklin and be back before their summer vacation is gone," Mrs. Taft said.

"We should get everyone together and sit down and decide whether we will all be going on the journey," John Shaw told her. "And we need to do that before we leave here in order to include Jonathan."

"Yes, that's what we should do," Mrs. Taft agreed. "I'll leave it up to you to arrange this, John."

"Yes, ma'am," John Shaw said. "As soon as I find out when everyone will be free at the same time for a few minutes."

"After we finish here and have coffee in the parlor would probably be a good time," Lindall Guyer told John Shaw.

John Shaw smiled at him and said, "You're right. And that may be the only chance we'll have everyone together in one room."

Mandie heard that arrangement and was

disappointed. She had hoped they could skip coffee in the parlor and go back to the old library and search for more information on the long-ago romance.

"Looks like our secret work will have to wait a little while," Jonathan whispered to her.

"Maybe we can make quick work of the meeting," Joe suggested.

"Quick work?" Mandie questioned.

"You know, we could all just say we have something else to do at whatever time they decide to go to Europe, that is if y'all really don't want to go," Joe explained.

"I would like to go back to Europe," Mandie said, "but not until we graduate next year."

"Yes, that would suit me just fine, too," Celia said.

"Well now, I'm all for the journey anytime you people decide to go," Jonathan said, grinning at the others. "I don't have any plans made that can't be changed."

"We really do need to get together on something before we go in the parlor," Mandie said.

Celia leaned forward to whisper, "Mandie, I just thought of something. Your grandmother said Senator Morton would be coming to your house after we go back. Do you suppose he will be going with us if we go to Europe this summer?"

"I just thought of something, too," Mandie whispered back. "Why can't Grandmother just take Senator Morton with her and go on to Europe without us?"

"Mandie, that would not be proper," Celia replied. "They wouldn't have a chaperon without us along."

"Maybe they will get married and move to his house in Florida, and then Grandmother wouldn't be around trying to make all the decisions for everyone," Mandie said, grinning.

"But then we would be stuck in the school all this next year without having her to go visit on weekends and all," Celia reminded Mandie.

"Y'all sure can come up with problems," Joe teased the girls. "Why not just say yes or no about going to Europe and forget about all the other problems? Or better still, why not just tell your grandmother that you would like to wait until graduation next year to go, Mandie?"

"I suppose I could," Mandie agreed. "We could go visit the Pattons in Charleston when we go home, and if Grandmother wants to go with us she could."

"And take Senator Morton," Celia added with a grin.

The young people had finished their food and looked up the table as the adults prepared to go to the parlor. Mandie and her friends stood up.

Mandie's mother, Elizabeth, spoke to her. "Come along to the parlor with us for a few minutes whether you want coffee or not. We need to settle this European date."

"You too, Joe," Mrs. Woodard said.

"And you, Celia," Jane Hamilton said.

As the young people stood up, Jonathan looked at his friends and said in a whisper, "My father didn't ask me to go to the parlor."

"You have to go with us, Jonathan," Mandie insisted. "Not only to help decide about Europe, but you just can't go back to that library and start searching without us. Please." She smiled at him.

"I suppose I could go with you all, but I warn you

I won't be staying in the parlor long," Jonathan replied, grinning at her as the four moved out and followed the adults.

As soon as everyone sat down in the parlor, Mrs. Yodkin came in followed by Monet with the coffee on a cart.

Mrs. Yodkin walked over to Mandie and said, "Miss, the cat has been fed and is in the kitchen."

"Oh, thank you, Mrs. Yodkin," Mandie said. "I just plain forgot about him when I left him in my room. I'll get him after we finish with our coffee in here. Thank you."

"He will be fine in the kitchen until you have time to get him," Mrs. Yodkin told her and went across the room to check on Monet, who was serving the coffee to the adults.

"I wondered where that white cat was," Jonathan said.

"We took your white dog for a walk with us yesterday," Mandie told him.

"Well, I appreciate that. Where did you go?" Jonathan asked.

Mandie told him about their walk in Central Park.

Then, as Monet approached them with the coffee, John Shaw spoke from the other side of the huge room. "Why don't all you young people move over this way so we can discuss the possibility of a journey to Europe?"

"Yes, sir," Mandie said as she and her friends went over to sit on a small settee near the adults. Monet served their coffee there.

Turning to Lindall Guyer, who was sitting next to him, John Shaw then asked, "Why don't you conduct our discussion since you most likely will not be involved in our plans, Lindall?"

"I'd be glad to, John," Mr. Guyer replied and sat up straighter in his chair next to Dr. Woodard and Dr. Plumbley. "I suppose the first thing to ask is, who would like to go to Europe?"

"I would, Mr. Guyer, but—" Mandie said immediately.

Her friends interrupted with, "I would, too." The adults nodded in agreement.

"Now that everyone seems interested in traveling over there, let's start around the room from my right and ask when you would be free to go," Mr. Guyer said, indicating Jane Hamilton next.

"I could arrange our affairs and go just about anytime, but of course the date would have to be agreeable with Celia," Jane Hamilton said, looking across at Celia.

Celia smiled at her mother and said, "Whenever you would like to go would be just fine with me, Mother."

Joe was next and said, "Don't let me change any of your plans. Just let me know when you settle on a date and I'll see if I can make it then."

Mandie was sitting next to Joe and said, "I'd like to go to Europe next summer."

Everyone turned to look at her. Mrs. Taft was surprised with this date and asked across the room, "Amanda, why wait until next year?"

"I've been thinking about going back to Europe, and I would like to go, but I've also been thinking that a journey to Europe would be the most wonderful graduation present I could think up. You had asked me what I wanted for graduation next year. And that's what I would like," Mandie replied.

"Oh, I see," Mrs. Taft said as everyone looked at her.

No one said anything for a minute or two, and then Mrs. Taft spoke again. "But, Amanda, we could go this summer and then go back again next summer. It's impossible to see everything in one visit, as you know from before. We could go to certain places over there this year, and then when we return next summer we could visit other countries." She looked at Mandie and smiled.

Mandie felt bad because she just didn't want to go along with her grandmother's plans, and she said the first thing she could think of. "Grandmother, we've already taken part of our vacation this year to come up here. I think we ought to go visit the Pattons in Charleston after we go home."

"To Charleston?" Mrs. Taft repeated thoughtfully.

"Yes, all my friends here would like to do that," Mandie added. "We could go just as soon as we get back home."

Everyone watched and listened.

Mrs. Taft finally spoke again as she looked around the room. "What do all the rest of you think about that, going to Charleston, that is, instead of Europe?"

"I wouldn't be able to go anywhere any time soon, so don't count on my input," Dr. Plumbley said.

"I'm afraid that applies to me, too," Dr. Woodard added. "I don't think I could stay away from my patients that long after taking time to come up here."

"Yes, that includes me, too, of course," Mrs. Woodard added.

Elizabeth looked at Mrs. Taft, smiled, and then said, "Mother, that would suit us just fine. We've been wanting to visit the Pattons."

John Shaw nodded in agreement.

Jane Hamilton smiled at Celia and asked, "Yes or no?"

Celia nodded with a big grin. "Yes, Mother, let's do."

Jonathan had not said a word, and now he looked across the room at his father.

Lindall Guyer smiled at him and said, "Now, if you are planning to go right away, I might just be able to go with you to Charleston. I have a few days I can take off."

"Thanks," Jonathan said with a big grin.

Mandie knew Jonathan and his father had very little time together because of the work Mr. Guyer did for the government. She could tell Jonathan was thrilled with the prospect of traveling with him.

Dr. Woodard spoke to Joe, "Son, if you would like to go with them to Charleston, go right ahead. You need a little vacation before you return to college."

"I was thinking . . ." Joe slowly began. "I hate to go without you and Mother, especially since I don't have much time at home anyway."

"Now, Joe, don't let that bother you," Mrs. Woodard quickly told him. "A few days on the beach down there would be good for you."

"A few days? They may be staying longer than a few days," Joe said, looking across the room to John Shaw.

"You can always go home anytime you get ready, Joe, if you don't want to visit as long as we do, and right now I'm not sure how long we plan to stay," John Shaw said. He looked across the room at Mrs. Taft.

"If we are going to Charleston, I can only stay

two weeks and then I need to get back home," Mrs. Taft said.

Mandie looked at her in surprise. Here she was trying to talk everyone into going to Europe, which would take a few weeks, and now she was saying she needed to get back home in two weeks. Could it be because Mr. Guyer had said he would like to go with them?

"Why don't we all go down together and return whenever anyone gets ready?" John Shaw said, looking around the room.

Everyone agreed to that. And now that their vacation was settled, Mandie was in a hurry to leave the parlor. She looked around the room. As far as she could tell, all the coffee had been finished.

Lindall Guyer looked at John Shaw and said, "Since Jonathan and I are going with you to Charleston, we might as well go back to North Carolina with you—that is, if you plan to leave immediately upon arriving at your home."

"Yes, no use in wasting any time," John Shaw replied. "What about leaving for North Carolina on Monday? Today is Thursday, and I believe the ladies would like to go shopping before we return home."

"That would be just right for me," Lindall Guyer said. "I'll check in with my office tomorrow and alert them I'll be away then."

Mandie looked across at her grandmother, who was talking to Elizabeth. Mrs. Taft had never promised a journey to Europe next year during all this discussion. Mandie hoped she had not decided not to give Mandie and her friends this for their graduation present.

"Come on," Jonathan suddenly said, looking at the young people. "I believe we can get out of here now. Let's go." He quickly stood up.

While the adults were engaged in various conversations, the young people hurried after Jonathan.

Mandie knew where he was headed. He also wanted to find out more about that long-ago romance.

Chapter 8 / Old Secrets

Mandie, Celia, Joe, and Jonathan returned to the old library to search for possible information on Mr. Guyer and Mrs. Taft. Most of the books were stacked double on the shelves, which meant there were twice as many books as shelves. Therefore, the young people had to take down two books at a time and try to keep them in order. There was a section on history, one on government, one on antiques, many, many fiction titles, and a large section of mixed subjects. It was a slow job.

"I would like to say we could move faster," Jonathan told them as he stood on the ladder to reach the top shelves. "However, if we don't keep the books in their original order, then someone might notice and wonder why these old books have been disturbed and then investigate."

Joe was on a ladder on the other side of the room, taking down books from the top shelves there. "I agree with you," he said. "We need to be sure to put the books back exactly where we found them."

"That's hard to do, because if you notice, a lot of them aren't in any special order, not alphabetically by author, or geographically," Mandie said as she and Celia worked on the lower shelves.

"Please be careful to look closely behind all the books to be sure nothing has slipped down behind them," Jonathan told them.

Mandie suddenly found a paper inside a large book. "Look!" she cried, opening the book. "There's a paper in here."

The other three came quickly to look as she pulled out the paper and handed it up to Jonathan, saying, "You read it. It is your property."

Jonathan quickly unfolded the single sheet of paper, scanned the page, and then laughed. "It's only a letter that came with the book from the publisher when my grandfather ordered it." He held it up for them to see.

"Oh, shucks!" Mandie exclaimed in disappointment.

"Oh well, we have lots more to go through," Joe said, turning back to the shelf he was working on.

Jonathan turned back to the top shelf where he had been examining the books.

After a while Mandie suddenly remembered that she hadn't been to the kitchen to get Snowball. "Oh, I forgot to get my cat!" she exclaimed, laying down the book she was holding. "I'd better go get him right now, if I can find the way."

Jonathan came down from the ladder as he said, "I'll go with you."

"So will I. I need a little break from all this hard work," Joe joked as he joined them.

"Then I'll go along, too. I'm not staying here in this strange room all by myself," Celia decided.

"All right, let's go," Jonathan said, opening the door and waiting for everyone to go out into the hallway. "Turn to your left here."

As they walked down the corridor, they discussed possibilities they might find in the old library. Jonathan had left the envelope with the clippings in its hiding place while they had searched the other shelves.

"Maybe we ought to get those clippings that you found back out, Jonathan, and look them over again," Mandie suggested. "Maybe we could get some clue about something or other from rereading them."

"I have looked at them several times, but I'll get them down for you all to see again," Jonathan promised.

"I wonder who put the clippings in there in the first place," Celia said thoughtfully as they continued down another hallway.

"I would imagine my father put them there when he was young and in love with Mandie's grandmother," Jonathan said, grinning at Mandie.

Mandie frowned and said, "Maybe they weren't in love. Maybe they were just good friends."

"I can't imagine escorting a girl all over town to all these social events unless I was in love with her," Joe said, smiling at Mandie.

"Well, maybe Mr. Guyer was in love with my grandmother, but maybe my grandmother was not in love with him. Knowing her like I do, I would say it just might have been a social thing for her, you know, a dependable escort."

Everyone stopped in the corridor and laughed.

"Do you mean your grandmother might have been keeping my father on a string just for social reasons?" Jonathan said, laughing loudly.

"I've heard of such things," Celia spoke up.

"Yes, and I do know my grandmother seems to be a social climber," Mandie said.

They walked on down the corridor and came to the kitchen door. Jonathan pushed the door open for the others to enter. There was no one in the kitchen but Snowball, who had evidently been asleep. He jumped up and began howling.

Mandie quickly went to unfasten his leash from the cabinet handle and picked him up. "Sorry I plumb forgot about you, Snowball," she said, holding him close and smoothing his fur with one hand. Snowball began purring loudly.

"That is a spoiled cat," Joe said, grinning at Mandie.

"You know, my dog, Whitey, has started acting like that, too," Jonathan said. "As soon as he sees me, he starts whining to get loose or come in the house. Do you suppose he's learning that from Snowball?" He laughed.

"Snowball hasn't been around Whitey enough to give him his habits," Mandie quickly said.

"Don't y'all think we had better get back if we're going to finish searching that library tonight?" Celia asked.

"Oh yes, let's go," Jonathan said.

"Since we will probably have to go shopping again tomorrow, which is Friday, and then y'all are going home with us on Monday, we don't really have much time left to look for any more information," Mandie said, following the others out into the hallway as she carried the white cat.

"I do hope we can find some answers to some of our questions while we have Mrs. Taft and my father together," Jonathan said as he led the way. "We might uncover something we would like to mention to them." He grinned at the others.

"You mean tell my grandmother and your father that we know something about them?" Mandie quickly asked in surprise.

"Of course," Jonathan replied. "In a subtle way, of course. If they know that we know something, maybe they would voluntarily give us some explanation."

"I wouldn't want to poke into Mrs. Taft's private business and let her know it," Joe said.

"Neither would I," Celia added.

"I'm not sure whether I would tell my grandmother about anything we found out or not. It would depend on what it is," Mandie finally said.

They came to the door of the old library. Jonathan pushed it open and waited for everyone to enter.

"Now, let's see what else we can find, if anything," Jonathan said, starting back toward the shelves he and been searching.

"Jonathan, let's look at those old clippings again and see if we can notice anything new about them," Mandie said, setting Snowball down after the door was securely closed.

Jonathan shrugged and said, "All right, I'll get them down." He climbed the ladder. Looking back down at Mandie, he said, "But you know we have a lot of territory to search yet in this room, so we'd better hurry."

"I know," Mandie agreed. "I just thought maybe with a fresh look at the clippings you already have, my mind might figure out something else while I work." She grinned at him.

Jonathan moved the books that he had removed before and then put his hand behind the other books to feel for the envelope. The others watched as he suddenly began quickly running his hand around the back of the shelf and then bent to squint between the books. "Now, I know this is the right place," he said.

"Yes, those are the same books you took out when you showed us the clippings," Mandie agreed.

"Maybe they fell through to the next shelf," Joe suggested.

"I don't believe they could have, because the shelves are built tightly with no cracks between them," Jonathan replied, continuing to reach into the space between the books. Looking down at Joe, he finally said, "How about bringing your ladder over here next to mine and let's just take all these books out of the shelves. Maybe I put them back in the wrong place."

"I was watching, and I know you put them back in the same place," Mandie assured him.

Joe moved his ladder over next to Jonathan's, and together they began taking out books and handing them down to the girls. There was nothing behind them.

"They have plumb disappeared," Celia declared as she watched.

"That means someone else knew they were there," Mandie said.

Jonathan looked down at the girls and said, "But no one ever comes in here or reads any of these books, that I know of, so how would they have found the clippings?"

"Maybe someone heard you talking about them," Joe said.

Jonathan suddenly hurried down the ladder. "Let's look around on this floor and see if anyone

else is around," he said, going to the door and opening it.

The others followed. He led them down the long
corridor, opening every door they passed and looking into each room. There was no sign of anyone
near.

"You know, Jonathan, someone could have gone
in the library while we were in the kitchen getting
Snowball," Mandie said.

"Yes, we were gone long enough for someone to
go in the library and take them," Joe added.

Jonathan frowned thoughtfully and asked, "But
who could it have been? I would say my father and
your grandmother, Mandie, are in the parlor."

"Let's check and see," Mandie said.

Jonathan quickly led the way to the parlor, but
when they came to the doorway, they stayed back
and peeked in so no one would see them.

Mandie stepped back to whisper, "Everyone is in
there." She saw her grandmother talking with Mrs.
Woodard. Mr. Guyer seemed deep in conversation
with the men. Elizabeth and Jane were talking
together.

The young people backed off out of sight of anyone in the parlor and discussed the situation in low
voices.

"Maybe it was a servant," Celia suggested.

Jonathan smiled at her and said, "I don't think
any of the servants would even be interested in such
a thing."

"I suppose all the servants are too young to have
worked here when my grandmother and your father
knew each other," Mandie said.

"Well now, let me see," Jonathan said, thoughtfully running his fingers through his dark curly hair.

"I believe Mrs. Yodkin's mother worked here when Mrs. Yodkin was a child, and also, Hodson is pretty old and could have worked for my grandfather. I'm not sure."

"You don't remember any old stories about Mrs. Yodkin or Mr. Hodson, do you?" Celia asked. "What I mean is, have they ever told you old stories about your grandfather and way back then when your father was young?"

"No, as you know, Mrs. Yodkin never talks much except business, and Hodson says practically nothing at any time," Jonathan answered. "But why would either one of them take the clippings?"

"Maybe they plan on blackmailing your father or Mandie's grandmother," Joe teased with a big grin.

"But there's nothing to be blackmailed now. If they were going to do that, it would have been when my father married my mother, don't you think?" Jonathan replied. "Let's go back and keep on searching the shelves. Maybe someone just moved the clippings to another place."

"That could be," Mandie agreed.

They followed Jonathan down the maze of hallways back to the old library. As they came to the door, Mandie saw that it was standing open and she rushed inside calling her cat. "Snowball, where are you?"

Her friends helped her look, but there was no white cat in the room.

Mandie stomped her foot and said, "I know we closed the door when we left. Someone has let him out."

"And there's no telling who that someone was," Jonathan said. "It could have been whoever took the other clippings looking for more because they knew we were in the room searching."

"You're right," Joe agreed.

"But, Mandie, we'd better look for that cat right now," Celia told her.

"Yes, you're right," Mandie agreed.

Jonathan quickly said, "I'll help you look since I know my way around. Joe, you and Celia stay here in case someone comes back again."

"If someone does come back in here, what do we do or say?" Joe asked.

"Just continue working on the books and give them the impression that you are looking for a certain book," Jonathan said.

"And if y'all find any more clippings or anything, don't lay them down," Mandie said. "Keep them in your hands till we get back."

"Don't worry, I won't let anyone take anything else while I'm in here," Joe assured her.

"And I'll help guard it if we find anything else," Celia added.

Jonathan led Mandie down several hallways, looking for the white cat. He opened all the closed doors for a second, peeked inside, and called, "Snowball," without any results.

Finally, Mandie asked, "Do you suppose he could have gone back to the kitchen, where the food is?"

"If someone let him out, they might have been carrying him, and he would have to go wherever they went," Jonathan replied. "However, let's check the kitchen."

When he pushed open the door to the kitchen, Mrs. Cook was there, cleaning up after her cooking. She looked at him and said, "Now, Mr. Jonathan, don't come begging. You had a right large meal tonight."

Jonathan laughed as he and Mandie went on into the kitchen. "No, ma'am, I'm not begging for food. We've lost that white cat and thought he might have come back here to beg for more food."

"I haven't seen that white cat in the last hour I've been in here," Mrs. Cook said. "And if he does come back here, I'll be sure to tie him up and send you word. Now, off with you. I've work to do."

"Thank you, Mrs. Cook," Mandie said as they stepped back out into the hallway.

"Let's continue our search," Jonathan said with a deep sigh.

Mandie smiled at him as they started on down the hallway and said, "I'm sorry, Jonathan, that you have such a big house my cat got lost in it." She laughed.

"Now, now," Jonathan replied, grinning. "Maybe we didn't close the door when we left the old library."

"I'm positive I did," Mandie replied. "I thought he would be safe in there until we came back. After all, you said the room was never used, so I thought no one would go in there."

"Oh, but they did, remember," Jonathan reminded her as they walked on. "Someone took the clippings. Therefore, someone has been in the room since I showed you and your friends the clippings earlier."

"You're right," Mandie agreed. "I'm just so disgusted with Snowball running off all the time, I'm not thinking right."

"But you don't know that he ran off," Jonathan said. "If you did in fact close the door, then someone had to open that door and let him out."

Jonathan had continued around the corridors until they were at the door to the glass room with the plants, and that door was standing open.

"Aha!" Jonathan exclaimed when he saw the open door. "We may have found that white cat. Remember when you came to visit before, he seemed to love this room with all the plants and kept going there?" He led the way into the room.

"Yes, that's right," Mandie agreed. She quickly walked around the dozens and dozens of tall plants, calling, "Snowball, Snowball, where are you?"

She suddenly heard a scuffling noise and started running in that direction across the room. She didn't see anyone, but there was Snowball sitting beneath one of the tall plants in a large pot, washing his face. He looked at his mistress and meowed.

"Oh, Snowball, how did you get in here?" Mandie exclaimed.

"Someone ran away," Jonathan said. "Didn't you hear that noise like someone walking on the cement?" He walked around the room, looking.

"Yes, but I instantly saw Snowball and figured I'd better grab him while I could. Which way did they go?"

"I don't know," Jonathan said. "I had the same idea as you, that we'd better catch the cat first."

"Oh well. As long as I caught him I suppose we'd better go back and let Celia and Joe know we found him," Mandie said, disappointed that someone had run away.

Jonathan agreed and led the way back to the old library. When he opened the door for Mandie, they were greeted by Joe and Celia excitedly waving papers in the air.

"We found more," Celia told them.

"And some interesting facts," Joe added.

"What is it?" Mandie quickly asked, setting Snowball down and coming to look at the papers they held.

"Wait!" Jonathan called to Mandie. Mandie turned to look back at him and he said with a big grin, "You didn't close the door. We may have to go on another cat hunt."

"Oh no!" Mandie replied, stooping to look for Snowball. He was curled up in a chair pushed up to the table. "Here he is."

"Thank goodness!" Jonathan said, firmly closing the door to the room. "Now, what did you find while we were gone? More romance?" He grinned at Joe and Celia as the two handed the papers to him.

Mandie came to read over his shoulder.

"Let's sit down. Some of this is startling indeed," Jonathan said, blowing out his breath as he sat at the table and spread out the papers.

Mandie pulled up a chair next to him and bent closer to see what he had.

"Oh my!" Jonathan exclaimed as he read. "This reporter evidently didn't like my father."

"Or my grandmother," Mandie added.

Celia and Joe pulled chairs up near theirs.

"Don't you think it's time we discussed these things and tried to come to some explanation?" Joe asked.

"Definitely," Mandie agreed. "I feel like asking my grandmother for an explanation."

Mandie wondered what would happen if Mrs. Taft and Mr. Guyer were confronted with their latest find. It would really be interesting.

Chapter 9 / Searching

While the four young people were still inspecting the papers that Celia and Joe had found, there was a light knock on the door. They looked at each other and silently stacked the papers and quickly pushed them back into the envelope.

The knock sounded again. Jonathan rose, walked over and opened the door, and asked, "Yes?"

Monet was in the hallway. "All of you are wanted in the parlor immediately, the ladies said," she told him and then moved to look beyond Jonathan into the library.

"We will be right there, thank you," Jonathan replied, glancing back at his friends.

Mandie stood up and stepped in front of the envelope on the table. At the same time Snowball suddenly jumped up from the other side and stepped on the envelope, causing it to slide off.

Monet continued standing there in the hallway. Jonathan repeated his reply to her. "We will be along shortly." And he closed the door in Monet's face.

"Now, what will we do with this?" Mandie whispered, stooping to pick up the envelope. She handed it to Jonathan.

"Yes, what should we do with this?" Jonathan asked, looking at the large envelope.

"Monet probably saw it," Celia whispered, looking at the door.

"How did she know we were in here?" Joe asked.

"She has probably been watching us all night and is probably still outside the door," Jonathan said.

"Maybe we could hide the papers somewhere and take the empty envelope with us. If she knows we have the envelope, maybe she will think whatever we found in it is still inside," Mandie suggested.

"That's a good idea, but where could we hide the papers in here?" Joe asked.

The four turned around and surveyed the room.

"Remember that someone took the other clippings. Therefore, whoever it was may come back looking for more," Celia reminded the others.

"But if we take the empty envelope and my father sees it, he might recognize it," Jonathan told them, turning the envelope over.

"But it's just a plain envelope without any print on it whatsoever," Joe said.

"And I know where we could hide the papers," Mandie suddenly decided. "We could put them under the carpet." She smiled at her friends.

The other three looked at her and also smiled.

"Now, that is a good idea," Jonathan said, quickly withdrawing the papers from the envelope and looking around at the carpet.

"We could move that chair there and put them under the corner of the carpet and then place the chair back where it was," Joe suggested.

"Yes," they all agreed.

Joe moved the chair, Jonathan slipped the papers under the carpet, and then Joe replaced the chair.

The four stood back and smiled. Jonathan picked up the envelope.

"I don't believe anyone will find them there, but as soon as we go to the parlor and can get away, I think we'd better come back and move them to another place somewhere," Jonathan said.

"Yes, but where?" Mandie asked as everyone started for the door.

"We'll have to figure that out. In the meantime, I don't like the idea of carrying this envelope to the parlor," Jonathan said, opening the door and quickly looking out into the hallway. "She is gone," he added.

"Couldn't you just stick the envelope in the hall tree outside the parlor door?" Mandie asked as they all stepped out into the hallway. She carried Snowball.

"We can sit where we would be able to see the hall tree from inside the parlor," Celia told them.

"And if we see anyone stop at the hall tree, one of us can just have an excuse to step out into the hallway," Joe added.

"Yes, I think we have it all planned out now," Mandie agreed. "However, we do need to do some thinking about the papers Celia and Joe found." They started down the hallway.

"We can discuss it as soon as we are able to leave the parlor," Jonathan promised.

When they reached the parlor, Mandie, Celia, and Joe paused in the doorway while Jonathan went behind them and slipped the envelope into the base of the hall tree, where the umbrellas stood. Then he joined them as they all entered the room.

Mandie's mother, Elizabeth Shaw, spoke from across the room. "Amanda, Dr. Plumbley is getting ready to leave, and I thought you'd want to say good-bye."

Dr. Plumbley stood up as Mandie hurried over to him. "But I'll catch up with you again before you leave New York, Miss Amanda," he said, and smiling, added, "the good Lord willing and the creek don't rise."

Mandie laughed and said, "I don't believe there is a creek between here and your house, Dr. Plumbley."

Dr. Woodard, John Shaw, and Lindall Guyer rose from their chairs.

"I'll just go out for a breath of fresh air with you, Dr. Plumbley," Dr. Woodard said.

"Yes," John Shaw said.

"My idea, too," Lindall Guyer added.

"Dr. Plumbley, we'll probably be gone shopping tomorrow," Mandie said, glancing at her mother. She held on to Snowball, who was trying to get down.

"Yes, Amanda. However, we won't be leaving for home until Monday," Elizabeth Shaw said.

"I'll see you sometime before then," Dr. Plumbley promised.

"Don't forget," Mandie said as the men left the parlor.

Then Jane Hamilton said, "Y'all sit down for a few minutes now. We've got to plan our day for tomorrow."

As the young people found seats near the ladies, Elizabeth Shaw added, "Yes, we need some kind of schedule so we don't all go running in different directions tomorrow."

"Elizabeth, don't count me in on your shopping expedition tomorrow. I have done all the shopping I plan to," Mrs. Taft said.

"But, Mother, if you don't go with us, you'll be left here alone for at least the morning, and I had thought we could dine out somewhere nice for the noonday meal tomorrow," Elizabeth replied.

"You just don't worry about me. I may have plans of my own," Mrs. Taft told her.

The young people quickly glanced at her and then at each other and smiled.

"That's fine then, Mother," Elizabeth said. Turning to Mandie, she said, "Now, Amanda, we have all agreed that we should leave as soon as we finish breakfast tomorrow, and by doing that we should have our shopping finished by noon and have the rest of the day free."

"And it's getting late, so, Celia, you should be getting to bed soon," Jane Hamilton told her daughter.

"You too, Amanda," Elizabeth added.

"Yes, ma'am," both girls answered.

"And, Joe, your father would like for you to go on an errand with him tomorrow morning while we shop," Mrs. Woodard said from across the room.

"Yes, ma'am," Joe replied. "I'm glad I don't have to go shopping again."

"But the little errand with your father may include a little shopping," Mrs. Woodard said. "Just be ready to leave with him immediately after breakfast."

"All right, yes, ma'am," Joe agreed with a frown.

Mandie looked at him with a smile. "You just can't get out of shopping here in this city," she said.

Jonathan cleared his throat loudly and grinned

as he said, "Well now, I don't believe I was included in all that shopping tomorrow."

"Jonathan, your father will tell you, I know, but he said he would like for you to join Joe and Dr. Woodard tomorrow since he will be tied up with business appointments," Mrs. Woodard said.

"Yes, ma'am," Jonathan said, grinning at Joe. "I'll be glad to get out of that shopping spree with the ladies."

Mandie, curious about why Mrs. Taft was not going with them and about what she had planned, asked, "Grandmother, do you not want to go shopping with us? You always seem to be real good at finding what we want."

Mrs. Taft smiled at her and said, "No, Amanda, there is nothing else I need to buy."

Mandie smiled back and couldn't think of an answer.

"Amanda, I think you should begin getting ready to retire for the night," Elizabeth said.

"And you, too, Celia," Jane Hamilton added.

The girls stood up and said, "Yes, ma'am."

Joe also rose. "I think I'll retire, too, if you'll just tell Dad I'll see him at breakfast."

"All right, son," Mrs. Woodard agreed.

Then Jonathan finally stood up to join his friends. "Well, since everyone seems to be retiring for the night, I suppose I should, too. I will see everyone at breakfast."

Good-nights were said, and the four young people hurriedly left the parlor. Jonathan quickly snatched the envelope from the hall tree and led the way down the corridor. He glanced at the others, put his finger to his lips, and said, "Shhh! No talking in the halls. You know why."

Everyone nodded. Mandie understood why. There was a possibility someone might be nearby and hear their conversation. And she was thinking there must have been an eavesdropper who had heard them discussing the newspaper clippings Jonathan had found and which had mysteriously disappeared.

When they reached the door to the library, Jonathan quietly pushed it open and everyone went in. He closed the door behind them and clicked the inside latch so no one could open it from the outside.

Mandie quickly put Snowball down and said, "The papers," as she started toward the corner of the carpet.

Joe moved the chair and Jonathan turned back the corner of the carpet.

"Still there!" Mandie said with a big smile as Jonathan picked up the papers and kicked the carpet back in place.

"Yes, but we weren't really gone long enough to give the thief a chance to do much searching this time," Jonathan replied. He took the papers over to the table, and everyone gathered around as he spread them out.

"There is no date on this clipping, so we don't know whether this episode happened before or after the other one you found before we got here, Jonathan," Mandie told him.

Jonathan laughed and said, "I would think this one was written after the other one."

"I agree," Joe said. "Their behavior in this one was so bad out in the public like that, how could they ever be seen together again?"

"Too bad this reporter was not sitting near

enough to hear what they were arguing about," Celia remarked.

"It must have been terribly embarrassing to your father, Jonathan, when my grandmother jumped up from the table and spilled coffee all over him," Mandie said with a deep frown as she reread the account of her grandmother's sudden departure from the table where she had been sitting with Mr. Guyer.

Jonathan grinned and said, "Well, I think he got even with her by grabbing the frill on her dress to keep her from leaving and then the lace ripping off." He laughed loudly.

"One of these days I think I'll tell my grandmother that I know about her public display of anger," Mandie said. "And all the time she has been telling me I should act like a young lady. I wonder what she would say if I created a scene like that."

"Mandie, you wouldn't!" Celia exclaimed.

Jonathan grinned and said, "Just wait until you and I are old enough to do the town. Then we can put on our own little show and be sure that your grandmother and my father know about it."

"And I will say I never heard of a girl named Mandie Shaw," Joe said sternly.

Mandie laughed and said, "By the time we are that old, we will probably have forgotten about this."

Celia looked at the other papers and said, "These other columns don't have any dates on them, either. I wonder if their friendship ended after that scene in the restaurant."

"Since they are not complete columns, we can't tell whether the same writer wrote these others or not," Jonathan said. "However, if it was the same man, I would say these others were written before that nasty one. He sounded like he was fed up with them for good."

"Jonathan, I was just thinking. Could it have been your father who took the other clippings you had found? Do you think he knows about all these and that they are hidden away in here?" Mandie asked.

"Yes, I would imagine he knows about all these clippings because he would be the most likely person to have hidden them here in the first place," Jonathan replied. "However, I wouldn't think he was the person who took the ones I found without taking these, too."

"Why don't we search a little bit more before we have to go to bed," Mandie suggested. "Tomorrow we will be out shopping and won't have a chance to do much."

"Maybe we could do one more section of the shelves if we all work together," Jonathan replied, pushing back his chair to stand up.

"What are you going to do with these?" Celia asked.

Jonathan reached back to gather up the papers. "Let's just put them back under the carpet for the time being." He stuffed them into the envelope.

"Here, I'll help you," Joe said, going to move the chair again and raising the corner of the carpet.

After Jonathan placed the envelope under the carpet, he turned back to the shelves. "Joe, you and I could do the top shelves and let the girls search the lower ones," he said.

"We had better work fast before someone finds out we didn't go straight to our rooms for the night," Celia reminded them as she and Mandie began on the bottom shelf.

The top shelves in that section were not stacked double like most of the others, so Jonathan and Joe quickly searched their way down and caught up with the girls.

"We only have one more shelf to go," Mandie remarked, indicating the shelf directly above the one she was searching.

Jonathan began on that shelf. Suddenly he stopped and held up an envelope he had found there. "This looks like the envelope I first found," he said, excitedly stepping down from the ladder to look inside the envelope. "It is."

The others gathered around to look as he held up the clippings from the envelope.

"That is odd, that someone would take the clippings and then bring them back and put them in a different place," Joe said, frowning.

"But we don't know that they ever took them out of here," Mandie reminded him. "Whoever it was might have just put them in a different place to confuse us."

"Anyhow, whoever it was must have read them," Jonathan said, turning the clippings over. "They are not in the same order I had put them in the envelope."

"Now that we have finished that section of shelves, I suggest that we quit for the night," Celia said.

Mandie looked at her and smiled. "You are right. We can't stay up all night searching this library."

"It is late," Jonathan agreed, hastily putting the clippings back into the envelope. "I suppose we should put this envelope with the other one under the carpet. What do you think?" He looked at the other three.

"Good idea," Joe agreed, going to move the chair one more time.

"Yes, that's the best place in here to hide something," Mandie said. "But, Jonathan, you could take all of it to your room."

"Oh no," Jonathan disagreed. "With maids running in and out of all the rooms all the time, the envelopes would be safer under the carpet." He stooped to place the envelope next to the other one. Then he pushed the carpet back into place.

Mandie reached for Snowball, who had curled up in a chair and gone to sleep. "As soon as we all get finished with errands tomorrow, do y'all want to come back in here and finish the other shelves?"

"Definitely," Jonathan agreed.

"We don't know who will get back to the house first," Joe said. "However, we could all check in here now and then to see if anyone else has come back."

"Yes, and you and Jonathan will probably be back first. I think my mother is planning for us to all eat somewhere downtown at noon tomorrow, so that will delay us," Mandie said.

"But we are supposed to have the afternoon free, according to your mother and my mother, Mandie," Celia reminded her.

Jonathan stepped over to the door and said, "Now, we need to be absolutely silent going down the hallway so if anyone is around they won't hear us."

The others agreed, and he silently opened the door. Jonathan motioned to the others to follow him as he showed them the way to their rooms. Once there, he went on down the hallway to his own room.

Once in their rooms, Mandie and Celia quickly got ready for bed. Snowball curled up at the foot of the bed and went back to sleep.

Mandie wanted to talk, but Celia wanted to go to sleep.

"I'm sorry, Mandie, but I am sleepy," Celia said with a loud yawn as she turned over on her side of the big bed. "Good night."

"Good night, Celia," Mandie replied.

Although it was late, Mandie was too excited to go to sleep right away. She had to rethink the whole story of the information they had found about her grandmother and Jonathan's father.

She wondered if her grandmother's parents were strict with her and whether they had ever known about the incident in the restaurant that the reporter had written about. Someday she was going to ask some questions in a roundabout way to see what she could find out. She didn't even know where her grandmother and her parents were living at the time the columns were written. However, if they lived in New York, the parents were bound to have known about the columns in the newspapers. What had they done about the incident in the café? Did they pack up and leave town in order to get her grandmother away from the gossip?

"Hmm," Mandie whispered to herself. Her grandmother had never mentioned living in New York.

There were lots of things she intended finding out.

Chapter 10 / More Information

The next morning the four young people gathered at the top of the main staircase to discuss plans before going down to breakfast. They sat on the chairs clustered around a small table there. Leila, the young maid, had already taken Snowball down to the kitchen for his breakfast.

"I wish somebody knew when we'll all get back today," Mandie complained.

"I have no idea where my father will be taking Jonathan and me," Joe said. "Therefore, I don't know when we'll return."

"And shopping with my mother could take all day," Celia added.

Mandie quickly looked at Celia and said, "I may know how to cut our shopping journey short. You and I can both keep telling our mothers we really don't want to buy anything else, or when they find something for us we could just say, 'That's fine.' Therefore, we won't have to spend time looking at everything in the stores."

"That might work," Celia agreed. "However, my mother may pick out something or other for me that I absolutely don't want, and if I say it's fine she'll buy it and I'll have to wear it."

"If you didn't like something, you could just take it on to school with you and hang it up and never wear it," Mandie told her.

"Oh, what a problem it is to be a girl," Jonathan teased.

A sudden rushing noise came from down the hallway. The four stood up to look. Angelina, Jens's ten-year-old daughter, came rushing toward them with Jonathan's dog, Whitey, on a leash. The dog was pulling her along as the cat chased the dog.

"Angelina!" Jonathan exclaimed, quickly stepping into her pathway and snatching the leash out of her hand. "Just what are you doing with Whitey up here?"

Mandie quickly stooped and picked up Snowball, whose fur was standing up as he growled at the dog. "Hush, Snowball, hush," she told him.

Angelina, pushing back her long dark curly hair, stood with her feet spread as she confronted Jonathan. "I am allowed to play with Whitey," she said in an angry voice.

"Not up here on this floor," Jonathan told her firmly, holding on to the white dog as he tried to get loose.

"I was going downstairs with him, and that white cat chased us," Angelina replied with a deep frown as she looked at Snowball.

"It doesn't matter about the cat. You are not supposed to be up here on this floor at any time, and neither is Whitey," Jonathan replied. "It was agreed when my father gave your father the apartment in the building next door that you were not to roam around in this house, and you know that."

Angelina pouted and wouldn't look at him.

"Where did you find Whitey?" Mandie asked her,

trying to calm her cat. "And where did you find Snowball?"

Instead of replying to any more questions, Angelina suddenly turned and ran down the staircase without even looking back.

"I have to take Whitey back outside to the garden, and I'll have to hurry," Jonathan told his friends as he started for the stairs.

"And I have to take Snowball back to the kitchen," Mandie said, following.

As Joe and Celia came behind them, they met up with Leila, who was rushing up the staircase.

"Oh, Master Jonathan, I've been chasing that girl trying to get that dog. Let me have him. I'll put him outside," Leila told Jonathan, reaching for the leash.

"Thank you, Leila," Jonathan replied, handing over the end of the leash. "That girl is not supposed to be in this house without permission."

"She was not seen, Master Jonathan," Leila told him as she went ahead down the stairs with the dog. "We watch to keep her out, but this time no one saw her."

"Leila, Snowball was running loose, too, chasing after Angelina and the dog. She must have let him out of the kitchen, where he was supposed to be eating breakfast," Mandie said as they all continued down the huge staircase.

"Yes, must have. I take cat, too," Leila offered as she stopped and turned back.

"Thank you, but I'd better take him myself. He's in a scratching mood right now," Mandie replied. "As soon as you get that dog out of his sight, he will calm down."

"Yes, miss, I hurry," Leila replied and rushed on down and disappeared in the corridor to the right.

"Let's go left here to the kitchen in order to avoid Whitey," Jonathan told Mandie, leading the way.

When they got to the kitchen with the cat, Mrs. Cook was surprised to see them. "Well, I never saw you take that cat. Last thing I knew he was eating breakfast over there," she said.

Jonathan explained about Angelina. "So she probably slipped in here and untied Snowball's leash," he said.

Mrs. Cook stepped over to the back door and flipped the latch. "I lock the door to outside this time," she said.

Mandie put the cat down at his plate, and he began eating. She firmly tied his leash to the handle of the cabinet door. "I tied him up, Mrs. Cook," she said.

"Yes, now he will stay and eat," Mrs. Cook agreed.

"We'd better hurry or we'll be late for breakfast," Jonathan said, turning to leave the kitchen.

"Yes, time to go to the dining room and eat," Mrs. Cook told him.

As he led the way out into the hall, Mandie saw the adults coming from the other direction toward the dining room door. "Oh, thank goodness we are not late," she whispered to her friends.

"Yes, we could have delayed everyone's plans for the day," Joe said, grinning at her.

"And my grandmother is not going with us, so it would be my mother who would scold us for being late," Mandie whispered as the young people fell in behind the adults and entered the dining room.

Everyone seemed to be in a hurry, and the meal was quickly consumed.

"Jens will drive me in the motorcar to my office,

and I believe the rest of you will fit into the carriage," Lindall Guyer said, laying his napkin by his plate.

"Yes, that would be fine if Hodson would just drop me and the boys off at Dr. Plumbley's office and bring us back when we are finished with our errands," Dr. Woodard said.

Everyone rose from the table as John Shaw said, "Don't forget I'm going with you, Dr. Woodard."

"Oh yes, of course," Dr. Woodard replied.

Elizabeth turned to her mother and asked, "Are you sure you don't want to go with us, Mother?"

"No, Elizabeth, I told you I do not need to do any shopping. I'll be fine right here while y'all are out," Mrs. Taft replied.

As they all went their way and Hodson ended up taking them to the shopping district, Mandie noticed they were going into the same store they had been in with her grandmother. As she and Celia followed the ladies out of the carriage, she said under her breath, "We've already been through this store."

"I know," Celia whispered back.

This time, however, the girls found the ladies leading them into a different part of the huge store. They went to the ladies' clothing department.

Mandie daydreamed about searching for the clippings as she and Celia followed their mothers and Mrs. Woodard through every section of the place. She was also wondering what exactly her grandmother was doing. She didn't believe she would just sit around the house while they were gone. Suddenly she leaned over to Celia to whisper, "I hope Angelina doesn't bring that dog back into the house while we are gone. My grandmother will be awfully upset if he gets near her."

"Maybe Leila or one of the other servants will be

sure he stays outside," Celia replied.

After looking at merchandise in every department and buying a few things, the ladies finally
announced it was time for the noonday meal and
that immediately after that they would return to the
Guyers' home.

"So now we have to decide where to dine,"
Elizabeth told the girls after they'd given the clerk
at the desk their orders for the merchandise, which
would be shipped to their homes.

Elizabeth and Jane discussed places to eat. They
were familiar with New York and its restaurants and
stores. Mrs. Woodard remarked that it was up to
them to decide, because she wouldn't know where
to go.

Mandie wished they would just go on somewhere, anywhere, and eat. They were wasting time,
and she was in a hurry to get back to Jonathan's
house.

When the decision was finally made, they had to
get Hodson and go in the carriage because it was
not near enough to walk. That took time in the traffic, and when they got there Mandie decided it must
be an awfully expensive restaurant. Her mother
ordered for her after the waiter recited the day's
menu in French. And when the food came, she
couldn't tell exactly what she was eating.

About an hour later they were finally on their way
back to the Guyers' house.

As they traveled through the heavy traffic,
Mandie told Celia, "I hope Jonathan and Joe are
back by the time we get there."

"I imagine they will try to hurry back, because
they are interested in helping us look for more,"
Celia whispered.

Mandie glanced at her mother, Mrs. Woodard, and Jane and decided they were not listening to the girls' conversation. "I hope we find more," she whispered back.

As soon as they arrived at the Guyers' house, all three ladies decided they would go directly to their rooms and rest for a while since none of the men were back. As they started toward the staircase, Elizabeth looked back at Mandie and Celia, who had sat down in the parlor. "Amanda, you should go relax a spell before teatime."

"But I'm not tired, Mother," Mandie objected.

"You too, Celia," Jane Hamilton said.

"I'll just relax here in the parlor for a while," Celia answered.

Mandie waited for a few minutes to give the ladies time to get out of the hallway and to their rooms, and then she said, "I'll go get Snowball from my room, and then let's go to the old library." She quickly stood up.

"I'll go with you," Celia replied as she rose.

Mandie found Snowball sitting up in the middle of Mandie's bed, washing his face. She scooped him up in her arms, and he stuck his tongue out to lick her face.

"Snowball, stop that," Mandie protested.

"He probably smells the food that you ate in the restaurant on your mouth," Celia told her.

"And I imagine he has been asleep all the time we've been gone and has not had anything to eat. I suppose I'd better take him by the kitchen and find out," Mandie replied.

"Yes, I would do that," Celia agreed.

When Mandie pushed open the kitchen door, there was no one there, but she immediately saw a bowl of food for Snowball by the cabinet. She set him down, and he raced for the food as she tied his leash to the cabinet door handle.

"I'll leave him here so he can eat and come back after him in a little while," Mandie said as she stood up.

"Do you think you can find the way to that library?" Celia asked as they left the kitchen and stepped into the long corridor.

"Let's see, now. I believe we go left here and then go right at the first cross hall," Mandie said as they walked down the hallway.

"If we had gone straight to the library from the parlor, I could have found it, but I'm not sure which way from here," Celia said.

The girls wandered up and down the hallways, but since all the doors along the way looked alike, they couldn't decide which one to try.

Mandie suddenly paused and said, "Here, this looks like the right door." She turned the doorknob and pushed the door open slightly. Glancing inside, she saw it was a sitting room and was about to close the door when she faintly heard voices from a connecting room behind it. Putting her finger to her lips, she looked at Celia and said, "Shhh!"

They stood there looking at each other as Mandie tried to figure out what the conversation inside was about and who was in there. Then her eyes popped wide open at Celia as she heard her grandmother saying, "I forgave you a long time ago, because after a while it didn't matter anymore."

Both girls held their breath as Mandie waited and listened for a reply.

"But it did matter a lot to me and still does," Lindall Guyer replied.

Mandie was afraid they would hear her heart beating, she was so excited.

"You know Sarabeth died about eight years ago, I suppose," Mrs. Taft said.

"No, I did not hear about that. What happened?" Mr. Guyer asked.

"She was thrown from a horse and died instantly," Mrs. Taft replied.

"How horrible!" Mr. Guyer exclaimed.

"I think I'd better get up to my room now and freshen up. The others should return soon, and it'll be time for tea," Mrs. Taft said.

"Yes," Mr. Guyer replied.

The two girls quickly darted down the hallway and tried several doors before they found one that was unlocked. They jumped inside the room and closed the door, leaving a slight crack so they could hear.

They were about to decide the adults had gone the other way when Mandie finally heard her grandmother talking as she passed the door behind which they were hiding. But the conversation was too low for Mandie to understand what was being said. She listened until there was no more sound and then quietly opened the door and looked up and down the hallway. There was no one in sight.

"We can go now," Mandie whispered to Celia, stepping outside.

"Now what do we do?" Celia asked.

"I don't want to go to the parlor, because we can't talk in there," Mandie replied. "Or the old library, either."

"Why don't we sit at the top of the staircase and

wait for Joe and Jonathan to come back?" Celia asked.

"That's a good idea," Mandie agreed. "Now, if we can find the right staircase."

They found the way up without any trouble and sat down in the chairs they had occupied that morning.

"Could you hear everything they were saying?" Mandie asked.

"Yes, I think so," Celia replied. "Your grandmother has long ago forgiven Mr. Guyer for something."

"Yes, something," Mandie agreed. "I wonder what that something was."

"It could be that incident in the restaurant, don't you think?" Celia asked.

"Yes, it could be," Mandie agreed. "But we still don't know what they were arguing about in that restaurant."

"They probably had lots of ups and downs if they saw each other over a long period of time," Celia said.

"You're right about that. My grandmother is not the easiest person in the world to get along with," Mandie said. "But who was Sarabeth, the person who was thrown from a horse?"

There was the sound of someone walking below. Mandie stood up to look down the staircase. She turned back to Celia. "It's Joe and Jonathan. They're back."

When the boys got to the top of the stairs, Mandie excitedly told them, "You will never guess what we happened on to."

Joe looked at her and grinned as he said, "I have

to go to my room first and put these packages away."

"So do I," Jonathan added. "But I'll be right back. Wait for me."

Both boys were carrying an armful of packages.

"So y'all did go shopping, too," Mandie remarked as the two went on down the hallway.

"Yes," they both replied.

They were back so fast Mandie knew they must have just dumped their packages into their rooms and hurried back to find out the news. They sat down on chairs nearby and waited.

"You didn't find more clippings, did you?" Jonathan asked.

"No, we haven't been in the library yet," Mandie replied with a big smile. "We've been eavesdropping."

"Eavesdropping?" both boys exclaimed.

"Yes, and here is what we heard," Mandie said, and she related the conversation they had overheard between Mr. Guyer and Mrs. Taft.

Both boys listened in surprise.

"Are you sure you didn't make this up?" Jonathan asked teasingly.

"It sounds about like that, sure enough," Joe added.

"Oh, stop teasing," Mandie told them. "Of course I didn't make it up. I heard it with my own two ears."

"Yes, we really heard it," Celia confirmed.

"Well then, if we could only find out who Sarabeth was, we might have a clue about what they were discussing," Jonathan said.

"She must have been someone your grandmother had kept in touch with for her to know what happened to her," Joe decided.

"And it was someone my father had not stayed in touch with," Jonathan added.

"I've been wondering if Sarabeth might have been the cause of that argument in the restaurant," Celia said.

"Do you mean you think that argument was over another woman?" Jonathan asked.

"Another woman would have been a good excuse for an argument," Celia replied.

"I see what you mean," Mandie said thoughtfully.

"Where is my father? I didn't see him when we came in," Jonathan asked.

"My grandmother was going to her room, so maybe your father went to his," Mandie told him. Then, looking at Celia, she added, "Maybe we had better go to ours and freshen up. It's about time for tea."

Celia stood up and said, "Yes, we should."

Mandie started to follow her but stopped and said, "I almost forgot. I need to go get Snowball from the kitchen and put him in our room."

"I'll go with you," Jonathan said, rising from the chair.

"And I will, too," Joe told her.

"Since I don't know exactly where we are in relation to our rooms, I'll have to go with y'all," Celia told them.

Mrs. Cook was in the kitchen, and she told them, "Almost time for tea."

"Thank you, Mrs. Cook. We'll just take that white cat out of your way," Jonathan replied.

Mandie looked at the bowl, which was now empty. "Snowball must have been awfully hungry," she said, untying his leash from the door handle.

"Yes, he eats good," Mrs. Cook agreed.

As they walked toward their rooms they discussed the conversation, but no one could decide exactly how it would fit in to what they knew already about Mrs. Taft and Mr. Guyer.

"As soon as tea is finished, are we going back to the old library to search some more?" Mandie asked Jonathan.

"Of course," Jonathan agreed. "The minute we can escape from the adults."

They all laughed as they went on down the hallway.

Chapter 11 / More Mystery

When everyone gathered in the parlor for tea that afternoon, Mandie and her friends held whispered conversations now and then as they watched Mrs. Taft and Mr. Guyer.

"They are ignoring each other," Mandie whispered behind her hand.

"With her sitting on one side of the room and him on the other, they act as though they don't even know each other," Jonathan said.

"At least they aren't arguing like they were in that newspaper clipping," Celia added.

"They're too old for that now," Joe said.

When they had almost finished their tea and sweet rolls, Lindall Guyer stood up and said, "Please excuse me for a few minutes. I'll be right back." He looked across the room and smiled at Mrs. Taft.

Dr. Woodard also rose and said, "If you're going outside for a breath of fresh air, I'll join you."

Mr. Guyer seemed flustered as he replied, "Ah, no, not outside. Just a little errand I have to do. I'll return shortly. Then we can go outside for that air."

Dr. Woodard sat back down as he said, "Fine."

Mr. Guyer quickly left the room. To Mandie's

surprise, Jonathan hurried after him.

"Jonathan," she whispered.

Jonathan turned to look back, shook his head, and said, "Right back." Then he disappeared into the hallway.

Mandie glanced around the room. The adults seemed deep in their own conversation. She whispered to Joe and Celia, "I wonder why Jonathan followed his father in such a big hurry."

"Maybe it was prearranged for them to meet and talk about something they didn't want to discuss in front of the rest of us," Joe suggested.

"Both of them said they would be right back," Celia added.

Mandie grew impatient for Jonathan to return after a few minutes. She debated going out into the hallway herself. Jonathan must know something he had not discussed with her and her friends.

"I could go get Snowball and look around on the way," Mandie told Joe and Celia.

"No, Mandie," Joe quickly replied. "That would be snooping into other people's business."

"Oh shucks!" she replied.

Before Mandie could think up an excuse to go out into the hallway, Jonathan returned, grinning as he came to sit by her and her friends.

"Guess what?" he said, still grinning. "My father went into the old library and locked the door."

"He did?" Joe said.

"But why?" Mandie asked, frowning at Jonathan.

"Why? What do you mean, why?" Jonathan asked her. "Evidently he didn't want anyone following him into the library. And you all should know, as well as I do, the reason he went in there. He's going after the clippings."

"Of course!" Mandie exclaimed. "You had said you thought he was the one who put the clippings in there in the first place."

"Yes, and he will know they have been moved if he remembers where he put them, which must have been years ago," Jonathan replied.

"Do you think he'll find any of them?" Joe asked.

"Probably not, because we hid them under the carpet," Jonathan replied.

As the four stayed huddled in their own group, they continued talking in whispers and occasionally glanced at the adults. The adults did not seem to notice.

"What do you suppose he wanted to do with them?" Mandie asked.

"Perhaps he intended showing them to your grandmother," Jonathan said with a grin.

"I wonder what my grandmother would have said to him," Mandie said, also grinning.

To the surprise of the young people, Lindall Guyer returned to the parlor after a few minutes, carrying a large envelope, which he placed on a table by his chair. Then he picked up on the conversation going on between the other men.

"Well!" Mandie exclaimed.

"Looks like he might have found at least some of the clippings," Jonathan whispered to the young people.

"I wonder what he is going to do with them," Mandie leaned forward to whisper to her friends.

"We'll have to watch and find out," Jonathan said.

Dr. Woodard stood up and, looking around at the men, said, "I believe it's time for some fresh air now." He looked directly at Mr. Guyer.

"Yes," John Shaw agreed.

Mr. Guyer rose and led the way through the vestibule out the front door. The women didn't seem to notice that the men were leaving but continued with their conversation.

"Look!" Mandie quickly whispered to her friends.

Mrs. Taft had risen and went over to sit in the chair vacated by Mr. Guyer. She stared at the envelope on the table for a minute.

The group held their breath, waiting to see Mrs. Taft pick up the envelope and perhaps open it. However, they were disappointed when Mrs. Taft rose and went back to her chair.

"Nosy," Jonathan said.

"Jonathan, can you tell if that is one of the envelopes we found?" Mandie asked.

"It looks like the others. However, they are all just plain envelopes, nothing unusual about them, and if you remember, the envelopes we found were alike," he replied.

The men came back into the parlor then and sat down. Mr. Guyer looked around the room at the adults and asked, "What do you say we all go out on the town tonight?" And then turning to Jonathan he asked, "Son, do you think you could entertain your guests while we are gone? You are all too young to go with us."

The four young people looked at each other and grinned. Jonathan smiled at his father and replied, "Yes, sir, we can find things to do here, that is, provided we have a big dinner of our own."

"All you have to do is tell Mrs. Cook what you'd like," Mr. Guyer replied.

"And where are you planning on taking us?" Jane Hamilton asked.

"Well now, I thought we'd start with the New York Dinner House and then move on to the Broadway Club for coffee." He looked directly at Mrs. Taft.

Mrs. Taft seemed shocked but didn't say a word. She glanced at the other adults, who were all nodding in agreement.

"Broadway Club? That's the place in the clipping!" Mandie excitedly whispered to her friends.

Jonathan nodded and grinned.

"Oh, I do believe they've kissed and made up," Celia whispered.

"I'm not sure about that," Joe said. "Mrs. Taft hasn't said a word about their plans for tonight."

"Oh, that would be a wonderful night," Jane Hamilton said.

"Yes, I would enjoy that," Elizabeth Shaw added. Then, looking at her mother, she asked, "What do you think, Mother? Sounds like an entertaining evening, doesn't it?"

Mrs. Taft seemed flustered and glanced at the others as she said, "Whatever y'all decide will be fine with me." She did not look at Mr. Guyer, who was watching her closely and then grinned at her reply.

"I wish we could go," Mandie quickly whispered to her friends.

"Sorry, you are underage," Jonathan teased.

"At least we'll have an opportunity to continue searching the old library," Celia reminded them.

"I suppose I should go to our room and decide

what I will wear tonight so I'll be ready on time," Mrs. Woodard said, rising.

Elizabeth and Jane both agreed as they joined her. Mrs. Taft finally stood up and asked, without looking at anyone in particular, "And what time are we expected back here in the parlor to leave?"

Everyone stopped talking and looked at Mr. Guyer, who said, "How about six, if that's not too early?" He looked at the ladies.

They all agreed they would be ready and waiting in the parlor at six o'clock, then left the room. The young people watched Mr. Guyer, hoping he would leave the envelope on the table. He got to the door to the hallway and then hurried back to pick it up.

"Oh shucks!" Mandie exclaimed as soon as he was out of hearing.

"Yes, I was hoping to get my hands on that envelope to see what's inside," Jonathan said. "But I suppose we should go to see Mrs. Cook now and order our menu for dinner."

"And then continue the search?" Mandie quickly asked as the four started out of the parlor.

"Of course," Jonathan replied. "We'll have enough time alone, with them all gone, that maybe we can finish and find something somewhere."

Jonathan led the way down corridors to the kitchen, where they found Mrs. Cook tying on a clean apron.

"And now, Master Jonathan, it's too early to come begging," she told him with a smile. "Nothing is finished yet."

"That's what we wanted to talk to you about. You see, my father is taking all the old people out, and it's just us kids left here for supper tonight," Jonathan began with a serious face. "And we'd like to save you the trouble of cooking a great big dinner tonight, because all we want is chocolate cake." He looked at his friends and grinned.

"Jonathan!" Mandie said, with Joe and Celia echoing her.

"You shall not have chocolate cake, Master Jonathan, unless you eat decent food first," Mrs. Cook told him, frowning.

"Like what?" Jonathan asked. "What would you suggest?" Turning to his friends, he asked, "Anyone got any ideas other than chocolate cake?"

"How about a nice big baked potato with lots of butter?" Celia asked.

"And some green peas with lots of salt and pepper," Joe added.

"And a piece of meat of some kind, ham or whatever," Mandie said.

"That makes a right nice order, it does," Mrs. Cook agreed. "So we will be having baked potatoes, green peas, and a nice juicy ham. Will that be satisfactory?" She looked at Jonathan.

"Yes, ma'am, that sounds just right, provided we have chocolate cake, too," Jonathan replied, grinning.

"It will be done, then," Mrs. Cook said. "Now skiddoo. Mrs. Yodkin will announce dinner when it is ready." She fanned her large white apron at them.

Jonathan bowed slightly and with a serious expression said, "And we do thank you, Mrs. Cook."

Everyone burst into laughter, including Mrs. Cook, who immediately pushed the door closed in their faces.

"Jonathan, I didn't realize you were such an actor," Mandie told him.

"I like to tease Mrs. Cook. She took care of me

when I was a baby," Jonathan explained as they started down the hallway. "You see, my mother died when I was a baby, and my father just turned me over to Mrs. Cook to raise. Then when I got too big for her to handle, she took over the cooking."

"That is very interesting," Celia said.

"I can tell she loves you, Jonathan," Mandie told him as they walked on. "She is not old enough to have been working here when your father was young and taking my grandmother out, is she?"

"No, she came with my mother when my father married her. Mrs. Cook had worked for my mother's family a long time," Jonathan explained.

"Oh, I wish I could see my grandmother when they go in that restaurant," Mandie said.

"I'd like to know what their argument there was about," Celia said.

When they got to the door of the old library, Jonathan stepped forward to open the door. It wouldn't budge. "It's locked," he said in surprise.

"Your father must have locked it," Joe said to Jonathan.

"Now what do we do?" Mandie asked in disappointment.

"I know another way to get into this old library," Jonathan said. "Come on." He quickly led the way down the corridor and then opened a door on the left and went inside. The others followed.

"This must be a storage room," Mandie remarked, looking around at stacks of boxes.

"Yes, it is," Jonathan agreed, walking across the room and opening a door on the other side. "This way."

He led them through several other rooms that seemed to be all connected. Finally, he opened a door, pushed a sliding panel aside, and there was the old library.

"Here we are," he announced, leading the way into the library. Then he stopped in surprise. The others gathered around him to look. There was Angelina sitting on the floor with clippings scattered all over the rug. "Angelina! What are you doing in here?"

The girl slowly got to her feet and didn't take her eyes off Jonathan.

"I asked you a question, Angelina," Jonathan said. "What are you doing in here, and where did you get all those papers?"

"You got them out of the shelves, and I wanted to see what you had found," Angelina told him, never taking her eyes off his face.

"How do you know we got them out of the shelves?" Jonathan demanded.

"I look through that door and see you all the time," Angelina said. "You look and look and find papers, so I look for papers and find papers, too."

"So you have been watching us all the time," Jonathan said.

"I didn't hurt anything. I just looked," Angelina replied.

"What are you hiding behind you?" Jonathan asked as she continued holding her hands behind her.

Angelina spread out her hands and said, "Nothing. Everything is right there on the floor."

"You are not supposed to be in here. Now get home immediately and don't let me catch you in this house again or I'll tell your father."

Angelina didn't say another word. She turned and ran through the door by which they had entered.

Jonathan quickly closed the door behind her and slid the bolt on it.

As everyone started to stoop and get the clippings off the floor, Mandie suddenly noticed something hanging on the wall between two sections of bookshelves. She rushed over to inspect it. "Look!" she told the others.

"I wonder where that came from. It wasn't in here before," Jonathan said, going over to where Mandie stood.

What looked like a large painting or photograph was entirely covered with a thick, rough cloth cover. The young people quickly tried to find an opening in the cover, but it was stitched tightly around the edges. There was no way to open it without tearing the cover off.

"I don't know what this is, but my father must have put it in here. I don't dare rip the cover," Jonathan said, finally standing back to look.

"Do you have any ideas as to what it is?" Mandie asked.

"I believe it is a picture, but of what I have no idea," Jonathan replied, frowning as he stood there looking.

"Your father probably put it in here for safekeeping and locked the door to keep everyone out," Joe said.

"I can't imagine why he would have a picture covered like that and locked up in this room," Jonathan said, frowning as he walked around the room.

"I have an idea," Mandie said. "Isn't your father still doing secret work for the United States government? Maybe it is connected with something that's secret."

Jonathan looked at her, thought for a moment, and said, "Yes, he's still doing secret work, but I've never known any secret work to be connected with something like a picture."

"While we think about that, why don't we go through these clippings that Angelina had and see if there are any that we haven't seen?" Celia asked, stooping to look at the papers on the floor.

"Let's do," Joe agreed. "We'll have to let someone know where we are when it gets to be time for supper, won't we, Jonathan?"

"We can keep up with the time and go back to the parlor when it gets close to suppertime," Jonathan replied. He sat on the floor.

The girls and Joe joined him, and they began reading and sorting the clippings.

Jonathan picked up some of them and said, "These are the original ones I found before you all came." He stood up and put them on the table.

The clipping about the restaurant incident was also on the floor, plus some new clippings they had not seen but which held no important information. They were just general gossip columns, and nothing seemed to have a date on it.

Jonathan stood up and said, "I just thought of something," he said. "If Angelina saw us put the clippings under the carpet, which she evidently did because they are all here, then maybe there are others under there, too."

Joe hurried to move the chair at the corner, and Jonathan lifted the carpet. There was nothing under it. They tried every corner in the room, but there was nothing else to be found.

"We haven't quite finished searching the shelves, so we probably ought to do that," Jonathan said, standing up to look around the room.

"I just thought of something, too, Jonathan," Mandie said. "Angelina could have put things in shelves that we have already searched."

Jonathan thought about that. "She said she had been watching us," he said. "So she would know which shelves we searched. Do you think she would go behind us and put papers in those?"

"Maybe," Mandie said. "Also, she may know who hung that thing on the wall there if she has been spying in this room."

"You're right. Now, why didn't I ask her?" Jonathan said.

"Because we didn't see it until she had left," Joe told him.

"Too late now. I'm sure she has left the house," Jonathan said.

They placed the clippings on the table and decided after a while that there were no more to be found.

"I think we'd better all go get washed up and meet in the parlor," Jonathan said, looking at his pocket watch. "Let's go back out the way we came in so the door will stay locked."

Mandie and Celia went to their rooms to wash up. Snowball was asleep on Mandie's bed, and when they came into the room he stood up and stretched.

"I need to take Snowball to the kitchen so he can eat, too," Mandie said.

"Let's hurry then and do that," Celia said.

They quickly freshened up. Mandie picked up Snowball, and they hurried toward the kitchen.

As they went down a cross hall and then downstairs, Mandie saw Angelina ahead of them.

"Look, there's that girl," she told Celia and hurried on.

Angelina had looked back and seen them. She turned a corner and disappeared. Although Mandie and Celia tried going up and down each cross hall, they could find no sign of her.

"We might as well leave Snowball in the kitchen and go on to the parlor," Mandie finally decided. "That girl is too hard to find."

When they got to the parlor after leaving Snowball, Jonathan and Joe were already there.

"Where have y'all been?" Joe asked.

"I had to take Snowball to the kitchen so he could have his supper," Mandie explained. "However, we just saw Angelina in a hallway before we got to the kitchen, but she got away from us."

"Let's take another look," Jonathan quickly decided and led the way back out into the hallway.

He knew his way around the house, and it didn't take long to search all the hallways, but Angelina was not to be found.

Later, after the evening meal was over, they looked for the girl again but without any results.

They went back to the old library and read the clippings until everyone got sleepy. They decided it was time to retire for the night when the huge clock in the hall struck midnight. Mandie got Snowball from the kitchen.

Mandie was too tired to stay awake and do much thinking that night. She soon went to sleep. She dreamed of the picture hanging in the old library. In her dream she was unable to uncover it.

Chapter 12 / From the Past

"Mandie, Mandie, Mandie, wake up. We're going to be late for breakfast," Celia was telling her as she shook Mandie's shoulder.

Snowball sat up beside Mandie, stretched, and then reached over to lick Mandie's face.

Mandie quickly pushed him away. "Snowball, stop that," she said, sleepily opening her eyes and then seeing Celia standing by the bed. She sat up and asked, "What time is it?" She yawned a loud groan.

Celia was already dressed. "Mandie, if you don't get out of that bed instantly, you won't have any breakfast. We have about ten minutes to get downstairs," Celia told her.

Mandie swung her legs over the side of the high bed and slid down to stand up. "Why didn't you wake me up in time?" Mandie groggily asked as she hunted for something to put on. She pulled down a blue cotton dress from the rack in the huge wardrobe.

"You were actually snoring, Mandie," Celia said. "You must have been awfully tired when you went to bed. I'll help you." She rushed over to the bureau drawer and took out a pair of stockings. "Here, put these on." She stooped to look under the bed. "Where are your shoes?" She found them and pulled them out.

Mandie didn't understand why she was so sleepy. She stretched and yawned and bent every which way and finally reached down to put on her stockings and shoes.

"We haven't had much sleep since we've been here," Celia told her. "We are used to ten o'clock curfew at school, and even when we're home that sleeping habit stays with us. It was after midnight last night when we finally got in bed." She ran over to the bureau and brought Mandie her hairbrush.

Mandie quickly brushed her long blond hair and tied it back with a blue ribbon Celia found in a drawer.

"I should take Snowball to the kitchen so he can eat before I go in to breakfast," Mandie said, looking at the cat, who was sitting at her feet busily washing himself all over.

"We don't have time for that. Come on. You can take him down later," Celia insisted, going to open the door.

Mandie was hoping Joe and Jonathan would be waiting for them near the landing, but there was no one in sight. When she and Celia got to the parlor, no one was there.

"Where is everybody?" Mandie asked as they looked around the empty room. She finally felt like she was awake.

"Maybe they're already in the dining room," Celia said, leading the way back out into the hallway and starting toward the dining rom.

Celia reached ahead of her to open the dining

room door. As the door swung open, Mandie was greeted by all her friends and family gathered around the table. "Happy birthday, Amanda!" they were yelling at the top of their voices.

"Birthday?" Mandie asked in surprise. "Is it my birthday? Why, yes, it must be, because today is June the sixth." She laughed as Celia guided her to a seat at the table.

"Happy birthday, darling," Elizabeth Shaw told her, coming around to hug and kiss her.

"Thank you, Mother," Mandie replied, squeezing her mother tight.

Lindall Guyer, at the head of the table, tapped on a glass and said, "Let's eat now, and we'll have the presents in the parlor."

"That sounds like a good idea to me," Jonathan said.

Mandie finally looked around the table at all the people. She almost turned her chair over as she saw Uncle Ned, her father's old Cherokee friend, on the other side and scrambled to go over to him.

"Uncle Ned! I'm so glad to see you," Mandie said as the old man stood up and hugged her.

"Happy birthday, Papoose," Uncle Ned said. "Number of years now fifteen. Must be young lady." He smiled down at her.

"Fifteen? Oh goodness, am I fifteen? I must be, I suppose, but that sounds so old," Mandie replied, laughing.

As she started back to her chair, she saw another familiar face. Dr. Plumbley was sitting near Dr. Woodard at the other end. She rushed down to greet him. "Oh, Dr. Plumbley, I'm so glad you could come back today," she said.

"I promised I'd see you again before you left New

York," Dr. Plumbley replied. "Happy birthday. You're getting to be a young lady now."

Joe spoke from the other side, where he was sitting with her friends. "Amanda Elizabeth Shaw, if you don't sit down and eat, we'll never get to that birthday cake, and I understand it is chocolate."

"Oh, I'll have to hurry for that," Mandie said, going back to her chair.

No one seemed to be in a hurry to finish the meal. Everyone was laughing and talking.

Jonathan leaned toward Mandie as he sat between her and Celia and asked, "Do we have to eat chocolate cake for breakfast?"

"Oh, I hadn't thought about that," Mandie said. "Why don't we save the cake for noon? Who planned this for breakfast?"

"It seems my father and your uncle John did, because this is the only time Dr. Plumbley could come," Jonathan replied.

"I'm glad he could come," Mandie said. "In that case, I suppose we had better go ahead and have the cake."

"I thought perhaps you could just blow out the candles and give Dr. Plumbley a slice to take home with him," Jonathan suggested. "I'm sure no one would want to eat chocolate cake for breakfast. We could have the rest of the celebration at noon. What do you say?"

"That's a good idea. Let's do it that way," Mandie agreed.

Jonathan got up and went around the table to speak to his father. Then Mr. Guyer stood up and said, "We will now proceed to the parlor for the cake lighting ceremony. However, if you don't want cake this early please don't feel obliged to partake. We'll have cake at noontime."

There were sounds of relief around the table.

When everyone entered the parlor Mandie saw the huge chocolate cake standing in the middle of the mahogany drop-leaf table. The table's leaves had been extended to take care of all the presents around the cake. She wondered who had done this while they were having breakfast. These things were certainly not there when she and Celia had come into the parlor earlier. Then she saw Mrs. Yodkin, Monet, Leila, and Jens standing at the side of the room smiling.

The candles on the cake were lit as everyone gathered around the table. Mandie blew them all out in one puff.

"I know that Dr. Plumbley has to leave, so he gets the first piece of cake," Mandie said, reaching for the cake knife. Her mother stepped up to help her as she dislodged the piece from the huge cake and put it on a plate without spilling a single crumb. She blew out her breath in relief. The first piece was always the hardest to get out in one whole piece.

"Thank you for coming, Dr. Plumbley," Mandie told him. "And I do wish you could come back to Franklin to see us and all the other friends you have there."

Dr. Plumbley accepted the cake with a big smile and said, "I will do that one of these days. Soon, I think, because we are all getting older. If I wait too long, you will be a grown young lady and away from home. And my old friends there are also getting older. I hope you have a joyous day today for your birthday and that the Lord will bless you in many ways, Miss Amanda."

Mandie reached to hug him. Her mother quickly took the plate from Dr. Plumbley to prevent the cake from being smashed.

Mrs. Yodkin, standing by, spoke. "I can put that cake on a plate for the doctor to take home with him if he is not staying, ma'am." She looked at Elizabeth.

"Yes, please do," Elizabeth told her, handing over the cake plate. "And, Amanda, since Dr. Plumbley has to leave, maybe you should open his present to you first."

"Oh yes, ma'am," Mandie replied, looking at the pile of beautifully wrapped gifts. Turning to the doctor, she asked, "Please tell me which one is from you."

"The small one there in white paper with the blue ribbon," he replied.

Mandie picked up the one he indicated and removed the ribbon and paper. Inside was a small book titled *Memories of Franklin,* by Samuel Hezekiah Plumbley. She quickly flipped it open and then looked up at the tall man and said, "Oh, Dr. Plumbley, this is such a wonderful present. I can't wait to read it. And I know everybody back home in Franklin will be wanting to read it, too. Thank you from the bottom of my heart."

Dr. Plumbley smiled and said, "Now, if you hear tell of anyone else back there in Franklin who would like one of those books, just let me know and I'll send them one."

"I can tell you right now you will be getting at least a dozen requests that I can think of," Mandie replied.

After Dr. Plumbley left, Mandie opened the other presents. There was something from everyone except her grandmother, and she couldn't understand that. Mrs. Taft had been unusually quiet all morning. Then the mystery was solved in more ways than one.

"Now that you have finished with those presents, Miss Amanda," Mr. Guyer told her, "let's go down the hall and get the one from your grandmother and me."

Mandie wondered why he was jointly giving her a present with her grandmother, but she smiled and said, "Yes, sir."

Mr. Guyer led the way, and Mrs. Taft walked by Mandie's side down the long corridor outside the parlor. He made a turn or two, and to Mandie's amazement he stopped in front of the old library door. Looking back at her, he said, "It's in here." He opened the door and waited for her and her grandmother to enter the room, with the others following.

Then, to the amazement of all the young people, Lindall Guyer reached up and pulled the cover off the picture that had been hung on the wall.

Mandie quickly looked to see what it was. It was a landscape of Niagara Falls. She stepped forward to read the artist's signature. "Sarabeth," she said, gasping, as she looked at her friends.

"Yes, Sarabeth painted this," Mr. Guyer told her as he glanced at Mrs. Taft, evidently waiting for her to explain.

"Sarabeth was my dearest lifetime friend, Amanda. We grew up together, went to school together, and moved in the same circles," Mrs. Taft said. "She was a very promising artist until her hands became crippled with arthritis and she could no longer paint." Her voice quivered, and she swallowed hard. Looking at Mr. Guyer, she said, "Lindall here was also in our circle until he and I had a terrible disagreement." She stopped and looked at Mr. Guyer.

Mandie could hear her friends take deep breaths behind her.

"This painting broke up the friendship between your grandmother and me because I did a very foolish thing," Mr. Guyer explained. "Sarabeth had her paintings on display at the museum, and this one was in the group. Most of the others were for sale, but Sarabeth refused to sell this one because it was her favorite and she was unable to paint anymore." He paused.

The room was so quiet, they could have heard a pin drop.

"Lindall and I both wanted this painting very badly, but I knew it meant too much to Sarabeth and would not even mention buying it," Mrs. Taft said.

"But me, I was a brazen young thing," Mr. Guyer continued. "I went back and talked Sarabeth into selling it to me for a fabulous sum. When I told your grandmother what I had done, she was so furious she never got over it. Our friendship was lost. And I was so upset by what I had done that I wouldn't even hang the picture in my house. It has been in the attic all these years. When your grandmother and I settled our old dispute, we decided to give it to you for your birthday. It's too wonderful a painting to keep hidden away."

Mandie grinned as she looked from her grandmother to Mr. Guyer and said with a laugh, "So that's what the argument was about at the Broadway Club." Then she glanced at her friends, who were all smiling.

Mr. Guyer quickly understood. "You've been

reading the newspaper clippings," he said. Turning
to her grandmother he said, "You didn't know I kept
all those columns. I thought they were well hidden,
but it seems these young people were smart enough
to find them."

"Amanda, I hope you never follow in my foot-
steps," Mrs. Taft said, smiling at her.

Before Mandie could reply, her mother spoke.
"Mother, I always knew there was something wrong
between you and Lindall, but I never dreamed it was
such a thing as this." Looking at Mr. Guyer, she said,
"I must read those clippings sometime."

"Of course," he agreed.

Mandie suddenly embraced her grandmother
and then turned to Mr. Guyer and hugged him. "I
don't know how to thank you both for such a present. I'll always treasure the painting."

Everyone in the room suddenly clapped and
said, "Happy birthday, Amanda Shaw."

Mandie turned to look across the room at all the
people. "I love you all," she said. Everyone returned
to the parlor.

Suddenly out of the crowd Angelina pushed her
way through, looked up at Mandie, and said, "I love
you, too, Mandie. Do you love me?"

The word caused tears to come into Mandie's
blue eyes. She stooped to hug the little girl as she
said, "Of course I love you, Angelina, a whole
bunch."

Jens, the girl's father, suddenly stepped through
the crowd and said to Angelina, "You are not supposed to be in here," he said. "You must go home at
once."

Before the little girl could reply, Mandie spoke
up. "It's all right. We are having a party, and I want

to give Angelina a big slice of cake to take home with her." She turned back to the cake. Her mother helped her slice a chunk of it, place it on a plate, and cover it with a napkin. Mandie held it out to Jens and asked, "Would you please carry it home for her so she won't drop it?"

Jens hesitated only a second and stepped forward to take the plate, saying, "Of course, miss. Thank you. Come along, Angelina."

"Thank you," Angelina called back with a big smile as they left the room.

Mandie thanked everyone for her presents again. Each gift was something she wanted.

As everyone finally settled down and found seats around the parlor, Mandie and her friends discussed the solution to their mystery.

"Imagine, breaking up a love affair for such a stupid thing," Jonathan said.

"It's good they did, Jonathan, or you and I might have been related somehow," Mandie teased him.

"This turned out to be a simple mystery, didn't it? No escapades to get us into trouble and all that," Joe said to Mandie.

"But think of all the years Mrs. Taft has lived through, detesting Mr. Guyer," Celia said. "Jonathan, do you think your father also hated Mrs. Taft all this time?"

"I don't believe they actually hated each other," Jonathan replied. "I think it was mostly regret for their behavior that broke everything up between them."

All of a sudden Mandie exclaimed, "Jonathan, you don't think they are still in love, do you?"

Jonathan grinned at her and said, "Could be,

could be. We'll just have to wait and see what happens in the future."

"And thinking of the future, maybe we can find another mystery when we all get to Tommy Patton's house," Mandie said.

"You are forgetting Senator Morton," Joe reminded her. "I would think your grandmother and Senator Morton are attracted to each other."

"Grandmother and Senator Morton?" Mandie replied and then said, "Oh well, we have thought that for a while anyway. And that reminds me. Senator Morton is going to Charleston to see the Pattons with us. So is your father, Jonathan."

Jonathan grinned at her and said, "May the best man win."

"It will certainly be an interesting vacation," Mandie decided. She didn't know then how interesting the vacation would be.

COMING NEXT!

MANDIE AND THE NIGHT THIEF

(Mandie Book/37)

Who could the thief be?

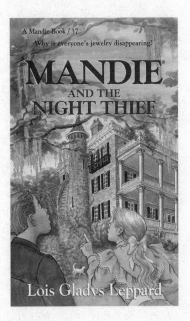

A Mandie Book / 37

Why is everyone's jewelry disappearing?

MANDIE®

AND THE
NIGHT THIEF

Lois Gladys Leppard